TOM SWIFT AND HIS ELECTRIC RIFLE

VICTOR APPLETON

Edition : Culturea (Hérault, 34)
Contact : infos@culturea.fr
Print in Germany by Books on Demand
Design and layout : Derek Murphy
Layout : Reedsy (https://reedsy.com/)
ISBN : 9791041953585
Légal deposit : September 2023

Tom Swift And His Electric Rifle

CHAPTER I

TOM WANTS EXCITEMENT

"Have you anything special to do to-night, Ned?" asked Tom Swift, the well-known inventor, as he paused in front of his chum's window, in the Shopton National Bank.

"No, nothing in particular," replied the bank clerk, as he stacked up some bundles of bills. "Why do you ask?"

"I wanted you to come over to the house for a while."

"Going to have a surprise party, or something like that?"

"No, only I've got something I'd like to show you."

"A new invention?"

"Well, not exactly new. You've seen it before, but not since I've improved it. I'm speaking of my new electric rifle. I've got it ready to try, now, and I'd like to see what you think of it. There's a rifle range over at the house, and we can practice some shooting, if you haven't anything else to do."

"I haven't, and I'll be glad to come. What are you doing in the bank, anyhow; putting away more of your wealth, Tom?"

"Yes, I just made a little deposit. It's some money I got from the government for the patents on my sky racer, and I'm salting it down here until Dad and I can think of a better investment."

"Good idea. Bring us all the money you can," and the bank clerk, who held a small amount of stock in the financial institution, laughed, his chum joining in with him.

"Well, then. I'll expect you over this evening," went on the youthful inventor, as he turned to leave the bank.

"Yes, I'll be there. Say, Tom, have you heard the latest about Andy Foger?"

"No, I haven't heard much since he left town right after I beat him in the aeroplane race at Eagle Park."

"Well, he's out of town all right, and I guess for a long time this trip. He's gone to Europe."

"To Europe, eh? Well, he threatened to go there after he failed to beat me in the race, but I thought he was only bluffing."

"No, he's really gone this time."

"Well, I, for one, am glad of it. Did he take his aeroplane along?"

"Yes, that's what he went for. It seems that this Mr. Landbacher, the German who really invented it, and built it with money which Mr. Foger supplied, has an idea he can interest the German or some other European government in the machine. Andy wanted to go along with him, and as Mr. Foger financed the scheme, I guess he thought it would be a good thing to have some one represent him. So Andy's gone."

"Then he won't bother me. Well, I must get along. I'll expect you over to-night," and with a wave of his hand Tom Swift hurried from the bank.

The young inventor jumped into his electric runabout which stood outside the institution, and was about to start off when he saw a newsboy selling papers which had just come in from New York, on the morning train.

"Here, Jack, give me a TIMES," called Tom to the lad, and he tossed the newsboy a nickel. Then, after glancing at the front page, and noting the headings, Tom started off his speedy car, in which, on one occasion, he had made a great run, against time. He was soon at home.

"Well, Dad, I've got the money safely put away," he remarked to an aged gentleman who sat in the library reading a book. "Now we won't have to worry about thieves until we get some more cash in."

"Well, I'm glad it's coming in so plentifully," said Mr. Swift with a smile. "Since my illness I haven't been able to do much, Tom, and it all depends on you, now."

"Don't let that worry you, Dad. You'll soon be as busy as ever," for, following a serious operation for an ailment of the heart, Mr. Swift, who was a veteran inventor, had not been able to do much. But the devices of his son, especially a speedy monoplane, which Tom invented, and sold to the United States Government, were now bringing them in a large income. In fact with royalties from his inventions and some gold and diamonds which he had secured on two perilous trips, Tom Swift was quite wealthy.

"I'll never be as busy as I once was," went on Mr. Swift, a little regretfully, "but I don't know that I care as long as you continue to turn out new machines, Tom. By the way, how is the electric rifle coming on? I haven't heard you speak of it lately."

"It's practically finished, Dad. It worked pretty well the time I took it when we went on the trip to the caves of ice, but I've improved it very much since then. In fact I'm going to give it a severe test to-night. Ned Newton is coming over, and it may be that then we'll find out something about it that could be bettered. But I think not. It suits me as it is."

"So Ned is coming over to see it; eh? You ought to have Mr. Damon here to bless it a few times."

"Yes, I wish I did. And he may come along at any moment, as it is. You never can tell when he is going to turn up. Mrs. Baggert says you were out walking while I was at the bank, Dad. Do you feel better after it?"

"Yes, I think I do, Tom. Oh, I'm growing stronger every day, but it will take time. But now tell me something about the electric gun."

Thereupon the young inventor related to his father some facts about the improvements he had recently made to the weapon. It was dinner time when he had finished, and, after the meal Tom went out to the shed where he built his aeroplanes and his airships, and in which building he had fitted up a shooting gallery.

"I'll get ready for the trial to-night," he said "I want to see what it will do to a dummy figure. Guess I'll make a sort of scarecrow and stuff it with straw. I'll get Eradicate to help me. Rad! I say, Rad! Where are you?"

"Heah I is, Massa Tom! Heah I is," called a colored man as he came around the corner of a small stable where he kept his mule Boomerang. "Was yo'-all callin' me?"

"Yes, Rad, I want you to help make a scarecrow."

"A scarecrow, Massa Tom! Good land a' massy! What fo' yo' want ob a scarecrow? Yo'-all ain't raisin' no corn, am yo'?"

"No, but I want something to shoot at when Ned Newton comes over to- night."

"Suffin t' shoot at? Why Massa Tom! Good land a' massy! Yo'-all ain't gwine t' hab no duel, am yo'?"

"No, Rad, but I want a life-size figure on which to try my new electric gun. Here are some old clothes, and if you will stuff them with rags and straw and fix them so they'll stand up, they'll do first-rate. Have it ready by night, and set it up at the far end of the shooting gallery."

"All right, Massa Tom. I'll jest do dat, fo' yo'," and leaving the colored man to stuff the figure, after he had showed him how, Tom went back into the house to read the paper which he had purchased that morning.

He skimmed over the news, thinking perhaps he might see something of the going abroad of Andy Foger with the German aeroplane, but there was nothing.

"I almost wish I was going to Europe," sighed Tom. "I will certainly have to get busy at something, soon. I haven't had any adventure since I won the prize at the Eagle Park aviation meet in my sky racer. Jove! That was some excitement! I'd like to do that over again, only I shouldn't want to have Dad so sick," for just before the race, Tom had saved his father's life by making a quick run in the aeroplane, to bring a celebrated surgeon to the invalid's aid.

"I certainly wish I could have some new adventures," mused Tom, as he turned the pages of the paper. "I could afford to take a trip around the earth after them, too, with the way money is coming in now. Yes, I do wish I could have some excitement. Hello, what's this! A big elephant hunt in Africa. Hundreds of the huge creatures captured in a trap—driven in by tame beasts. Some are shot for their tusks. Others will be sent to museums."

He was reading the headlines of the article that had attracted his attention, and, as he read, he became more and more absorbed in it. He read the story through twice, and then, with sparkling eyes, he exclaimed:

"That's just what I want. Elephant shooting in Africa! My! With my new electric rifle, and an airship, what couldn't a fellow do over in the dark continent! I've a good notion to go there! I wonder if Ned would go with me? Mr. Damon certainly would. Elephant shooting in Africa! In an airship! I could finish my new sky craft in short order if I wanted to. I've a good notion to do it!"

CHAPTER II

TRYING THE NEW GUN

While Tom Swift is thus absorbed in thinking about a chance to hunt elephants, we will take the opportunity to tell you a little more about him, and then go on with the story.

Many of you already know the young inventor, but those who do not may be interested in hearing that he is a young American lad, full of grit and ginger, who lives with his aged father in the town of Shopton, in New York State. Our hero was first introduced to the public in the book, "Tom Swift and His Motorcycle."

In that volume it was related how Tom bought a motor-cycle from a Mr. Wakefield Damon, of Waterford. Mr. Damon was an eccentric individual, who was continually blessing himself, some one else, or something belonging to him. His motor-cycle tried to climb a tree with him, and that was why he sold it to Tom. The two thus became acquainted, and their friendship grew from year to year.

After many adventures on his motor-cycle Tom got a motor-boat, and had some exciting times in that. One of the things he and his father and his chum, Ned Newton, did, was to rescue, from a burning balloon that had fallen into Lake Carlopa, an aeronaut named John Sharp. Later Tom and Mr. Sharp built an airship called the Red Cloud, and with Mr. Damon and some others had a series of remarkable fights.

In the Red Cloud they got on the track of some bank robbers, and captured them, thus foiling the plans of Andy Foger, a town bully, and one of Tom's enemies, and putting to confusion the plot of Mr. Foger, Andy's father.

After many adventures in the air Tom and his friends, in a submarine boat, invented by Mr. Swift, went under the ocean for sunken treasure and secured a large part of it.

It was not long after this that Tom conceived the idea of a powerful electric car, which proved, to be the speediest of the road, and in it he won a great race, and saved from ruin a bank in which his father and Mr. Damon were interested.

The sixth book of the series, entitled "Tom Swift and His Wireless Message," tells how, in testing a new electric airship, which a friend of Mr. Damon's had invented, Tom, the inventor and Mr. Damon were lost on an island in the middle of the ocean. There they found some castaways, among whom were Mr. and Mrs. Nestor, parents of Mary Nestor of Shopton, a girl of whom Tom was quite fond.

Tom Swift, after his arrival home, went on an expedition among a gang of men known as the "Diamond Makers" who were hidden in the Rocky Mountains. He was accompanied by Mr. Barcoe Jenks, one of the castaways of Earthquake Island. They found the diamond makers, and had some surprising adventures, barely escaping with their lives.

This did not daunt Tom, however, and he once more started off on an expedition in his airship the Red Cloud to Alaska, amid the caves of ice. He was searching for a valley of gold, and though he and his friends found it, they came to grief. The Fogers, father and son, tried to steal the gold from them, and, failing in that, incited the Eskimos against our friends. There was a battle, but the forces of nature were even more to be dreaded than the terrible savages.

The ice cave, in which the Red Cloud was stored, collapsed, crushing the gallant craft, and burying it out of sight forever under thousand of tons of the frozen bergs.

After a desperate journey Tom and his friends reached civilization, with a large supply of gold. Tom regretted very much the destruction of the airship, but he at once set to work on another—a monoplane this time, instead of a combined aeroplane and dirigible balloon. This new craft he called the Humming-Bird and it was a "sky racer" of terrific speed. In it, as we have said, Tom brought a specialist to operate on his father, when, because of a broken railroad bridge, the physician could not otherwise have gotten to Shopton. He and Tom traveled through the air at the rate of over one hundred miles an hour. Later, Tom took part in a big race for a ten-thousand-dollar prize, and won, defeating Andy Foger, and a number of well-known "bird-men" who used biplanes and monoplanes of a more or less familiar type.

The government became interested in Tom's craft, the Humming-Bird, and, as told in the ninth book of this series, Tom Swift and His Sky Racer, they secured some rights in the invention.

And now Tom, who had done nothing for several months following the great race—that is, nothing save to work on his new rifle—Tom, we say, sighed for new adventures.

"Well, Tom, what is on your mind?" asked his father at the supper table that evening. "What is worrying you?"

"Nothing is worrying me, Dad."

"You are thinking of something. I can see that. Are you afraid your electric rifle won't work as well as you hope, when Ned comes over to try it?"

"No, it isn't that, Dad. But I may as well tell you, I guess. I've been reading in the paper about a big elephant hunt in Africa, and I—"

"That's enough, Tom! You needn't say any more," interrupted Mr. Swift. "I can see which way the wind is blowing. You want to go to Africa with your new rifle."

"Well, Dad, not exactly—that is—"

"Now, Tom, you needn't deny it," and Mr. Swift laughed. "Well, I don't blame you a bit. You have been rather idle of late."

"I would like to go, Dad," admitted the young inventor, "only I'd never think of it while you weren't well."

"Don't worry about me, Tom. Of course I will be lonesome while you are gone, but don't let that stand in the way. If you want to go to Africa, you may start to-morrow, and take your new rifle with you."

"The rifle part would be all right, Dad, but if I went I'd want to take an airship along, and it will take me some little time to finish the Black Hawk, as I have named my new craft."

"Well, there's no special hurry, is there?" asked Mr. Swift. "The elephants in Africa are likely to stay there for some time. If you want to go, why don't you get right to work on the Black Hawk and make the trip? I'd like to go myself."

"I wish you would, Dad," exclaimed Tom eagerly.

"No, son, I couldn't think of it. I want to stay here and get well. Then I am going to resume work on my wireless motor. Perhaps I'll have it finished when you come back from Africa with an airship load of elephants' tusks."

"Perhaps," admitted the young inventor. "Well, Dad, I'll think of it. But now I'm going after my rifle, and—"

Tom was interrupted by a ring of the front-door bell, and Mrs. Baggert, the housekeeper, who was almost like a mother to the youth, went to answer it.

"It's Ned Newton, I guess," murmured Tom, and, a little later, his chum entered the room.

"Oh, I guess I'm early," said Ned. "Haven't you had supper yet, Tom?"

"Yes, we're just finished. Come on out and we'll try the gun."

"And practice shooting elephants," added Mr. Swift with a laugh, as he mentioned to Ned the latest idea of Tom.

"Say! That would be great!" cried the bank clerk. "I wish I could go!"

"Come along!" invited Tom cordially. "We'll have more fun than we did in the caves of ice," for Ned had gone on the voyage to Alaska.

The two youths went out to the shed where the rifle gallery had been built. The new electric weapon was out there, and Eradicate Sampson, the colored man, who was a sort of servant and man-of-all-work about the Swift household, had set up the scarecrow figure at the end of the gallery.

"Now we'll try some shots," said Tom, as he took the gun out of the case. "Just turn on a few more lights, will you, Mr. Jackson," and the engineer, who was employed by Tom and his father to aid them in their inventive work, did as requested.

The gallery was now brilliantly illuminated, with the reflectors throwing the beams on the big stuffed figure, which, save for a face, looked very much like a human being, standing at the end of the gallery.

"I don't suppose you want to go down there and hold it, while I shoot at it; do you, Rad?" asked Tom jokingly, as he prepared the electric rifle for use.

"No indeedy, I don't!" cried Eradicate. "Yo'-all will hab t' scuse me, Massa Tom. I think I'll be goin' now."

"What's your hurry?" asked Ned, as he saw the colored man hastily preparing to leave the improvised gallery.

"I spects I'd better fro' down some mo' straw fo' a bed fo' my mule Boomerang!" exclaimed Eradicate, as he hastily slid out of the door, and shut it after him.

"Rad is nervous," remarked Tom. "He doesn't like this gun. Well, it certainly does great execution."

"How does it work'" asked Ned, as he looked at the curious gun. The electric weapon was not unlike an ordinary heavy rifle in appearance save that the barrel was a little longer, and the stock larger in every way. There were also a number of wheels, levers, gears and gages on the stock.

"It works by electricity," explained Tom.

"That is, the force comes from a powerful current of stored electricity."

"Oh, then you have storage batteries in the stock?"

"Not exactly. There are no batteries, but the current is a sort of wireless kind. It is stored in a cylinder, just as compressed air or gases are stored, and can be released as I need it."

"And when it's all gone, what do you do?"

"Make more power by means of a small dynamo."

"And does it shoot lead bullets?"

"Not at all. There are no bullets used."

"Then how does it kill?"

"By means of a concentrated charge of electricity which is shot from the barrel with great force. You can't see it, yet it is there. It's just as if you concentrated a charge of electricity of five thousand volts into a small globule the size of a bullet. That flies through space, strikes the object aimed at and—well, we'll see what it does in a minute. Mr. Jackson, just put that steel plate up in front of the scarecrow; will you?"

The engineer proceeded to put into place a section of steel armor- plate before the stuffed figure.

"You don't mean to say you're going to shoot through that, do you?" asked Ned in surprise.

"Surely. The electric bullets will pierce anything. They'll go through a brick wall as easily as the x-rays do. That's one valuable feature of my rifle. You don't have to see the object you aim at. In fact you can fire through a house, and kill something on the other side."

"I should think that would be dangerous."

"It would be, only I can calculate exactly, by means of an automatic arrangement, just how far the charge of electricity will go. It stops short just at the limit of the range, and is not effective beyond that. Otherwise, if I did not limit it and if I fired at the scarecrow, through the piece of steel, and the bullet hit the figure, it would go on, passing through whatever else was in the way, until its power was lost. I use the term 'bullet,' though as I said, it isn't properly one."

"By Jove, Tom, it certainly is a dangerous weapon!"

"Yes, the range-limit idea is a new one. That's what I've been working on lately. There are other features of the gun which I'll explain later, particularly the power it has to shoot out luminous bars of light. But now we'll see what it will do to the image."

Tom took his place at the end of the range, and began to adjust some valves and levers. In spite of the fact that the gun was larger than an ordinary rifle, it was not as heavy as the United States Army weapon.

Tom aimed at the armor-plate, and, by means of an arrangement on the rifle, he could tell exactly when he was pointing at the scarecrow, even though he could not see it.

"Here she goes!" he suddenly exclaimed.

Ned watched his chum. The young inventor pressed a small button at the side of the rifle barrel, about where the trigger should have been. There was no sound, no smoke, no flame and not the slightest jar.

Yet as Ned watched he saw the steel plate move slightly. The next instant the scarecrow figure seemed to fly all to pieces. There was a shower of straw, rags and old clothes, which fell in a shapeless heap at the end of the range.

"Say. I guess you did for that fellow, all right!" exclaimed Ned.

"It looks so," admitted Tom, with a note of pride in his voice. "Now we'll try another test."

As he laid aside his rifle in order to help Mr. Jackson shift the steel plate there was a series of yells outside the shed.

"What's that?" asked Tom, in some alarm.

"Sounds like some one calling," answered Ned.

"It is," agreed Mr. Jackson. "Perhaps Eradicate's mule has gotten loose. I guess we'd better—"

He did not finish, for the shouts increased in volume, and Tom and Ned could hear some one yelling:

"I'll have the law on you for this! I'll have you arrested, Tom Swift! What do you mean by trying to kill me? Where are you? Don't try to hide away, now. You were trying to shoot me, and I'm not going to have it!"

Some one pounded on the door of the shed.

"It's Barney Moker!" exclaimed Tom. "I wonder what can have happened?"

CHAPTER III

A DIFFICULT TEST

Tom Swift opened the door of the improvised rifle gallery and looked out. By the light of a full moon, which shone down from a cloudless sky, he saw a man standing at the portal. The man's face was distorted with rage, and he shook his fist at the young inventor.

"What do you mean by shooting at me?" he demanded. "What do you mean, I say? The idea of scaring honest folks out of their wits, and making 'em think the end of the world has come! What do you mean by it? Why don't you answer me? I say, Tom Swift, why don't you answer me?"

"Because you don't give me a chance, Mr. Moker," replied our hero.

"I want to know why you shot at me? I demand to know!" and Mr. Moker, who was a sort of miserly town character, living all alone in a small house, just beyond Tom's home, again shook his fist almost in the lad's face. "Why don't you tell me? Why don't you tell me?" he shouted.

"I will, if you give me a chance!" fairly exploded Tom. "If you can be cool for five minutes, and come inside and tell me what happened I'll be glad to answer any of your questions, Mr. Moker. I didn't shoot at you."

"Yes, you did! You tried to shoot a hole through me!"

"Tell me about it?" suggested Tom, as the excited man calmed down somewhat. "Are you hurt?"

"No, but it isn't your fault that I'm not. You tried hard enough to hurt me. Here I am, sitting at my table reading, and, all at once something goes through the side of the house, whizzes past my ear, makes my hair fairly stand up on end, and goes outside the other side of the house. What kind of bullets do you use, Tom Swift? that's what I want to know. They went through the side of my house, and never left a mark. I demand to know what kind they are."

"I'll tell you, if you'll only give me a chance," went on Tom wearily. "How do you know it was me shooting?"

"How do I know? Why, doesn't the end of this shooting gallery of yours point right at my house? Of course it does; you can't deny it!"

Tom did not attempt to, and Mr. Moker went on:

"Now what do you mean by it?"

"If any of the bullets from my electric gun went near you, it was a mistake, and I'm sorry for it," said Tom.

"Well, they did, all right," declared the excited man. "They went right past my ear."

"I don't see how they could," declared Tom. "I was trying my new electric rifle, but I had the limit set for two hundred feet, the length of the gallery. That is, the electrical discharge couldn't go beyond that distance."

"I don't know what it was, but it went through the side of my house all the same," insisted Mr. Moker. "It didn't make a hole, but it scorched the wall paper a little."

"I don't see how it could," declared Tom. "It couldn't possibly have gone over two hundred feet with the gage set for that distance." He paused suddenly, and hurried over to where he had placed his gun. Catching up the weapon he looked at the gage dial. Then he uttered an exclamation.
"I'm sorry to admit that you are right, Mr. Moker!" he said finally. "I made a mistake. The gage is set for a thousand feet instead of two hundred. I forgot to change it. The charge, after passing through the steel plate, and the scarecrow figure, destroying the latter, went on, and shot through the side of your house."
"Ha! I knew you were trying to shoot me!" exclaimed the still angry man. "I'll have the law on you for this!"
"Oh, that's all nonsense!" broke in Ned Newton "Everybody knows Tom Swift wouldn't try to shoot you, or any one else, Mr. Moker."
"Then why did he shoot at me?"
"That was a mistake," explained Tom, "and I apologize to you for it."
"Humph! A lot of good that would do me, if I'd been killed!" muttered the miser. "I'm going to sue you for this. You might have put me in my grave."
"Impossible!" exclaimed Tom.
"Why impossible?" demanded the visitor.
"Because I had so set the rifle that almost the entire force of the electrical bullet was expended in blowing apart the scarecrow figure I made for a test," explained Tom. "All that passed through your house was a small charge, and, if it HAD hit you there would have been no more than a little shock, such as you would feel in taking hold of an electric battery."
"How do I know this?" asked the man cunningly. "You say so, but for all I know you may have wanted to kill me."
"Why?" asked Tom, trying not to laugh.
"Oh, so you might get some of my money. Of course I ain't got none," the miser went on quickly, "but folks thinks I've got a lot, and I have to be on the lookout all the while, or they'd murder me for it."
"I wouldn't," declared the young inventor. "It was a mistake. Only part of the spent charge passed near you. Why, if it had been a powerful charge you would never have been able to come over here. I set the main charge to go off inside the scarecrow, and it did so, as you can see by looking at what's left of it," and he pointed to the pile of clothes and rags.
"How do I know this?" insisted the miser with a leer at the two lads.
"Because if the charge had gone off either before or after it passed through the figure, it would not have caused such havoc of the cloth and straw," explained Tom. "First the charge would have destroyed the steel plate, which it passed through without even denting it. Why, look here, I will now fire the rifle at short range, and set it to destroy the plate. See what happens."

He quickly adjusted the weapon, and aimed it at the plate, which, had again been set up on the range. This time Tom was careful to set the gage so that even a small part of the spent charge would not go outside the gallery.

The young inventor pressed the button, and instantly the heavy steel plate was bent, torn and twisted as though a small sized cannon ball had gone through it.

"That's what the rifle will do at short range," said Tom. "Don't worry, Mr. Moker, you didn't have a narrow escape. You were in no danger at all, though I apologize for the fright I caused you."

"Humph! That's an easy way to get out of it!" exclaimed the miser. "I believe I could sue you for damages, anyhow. Look at my scorched wall paper."

"Oh, I'll pay for that," said Tom quickly, for he did not wish to have trouble with the unpleasant man. "Will ten dollars be enough?" He knew that the whole room could be repapered for that, and he did not believe the wall-covering was sufficiently damaged for such work to be necessary.

"Well, if you'll make it twelve dollars, I won't say anything more about it," agreed the miser craftily, "though it's worth thirteen dollars, if it is a penny. Give me twelve dollars, Tom Swift, and I won't prosecute you."

"All right, twelve dollars it shall be," responded the young inventor, passing over the money, and glad to be rid of the unpleasant character.

"And after this, just fire that gun of yours the other way," suggested Mr. Moker as he went out, carefully folding the bills which Tom had handed him.

"Hum! that was rather queer," remarked Ned, after a pause.

"It sure was," agreed his chum. "This rifle will do more than I thought it would. I'll have to be more careful. I was sure I set the gage for two hundred feet. I'll have to invent some automatic attachment to prevent it being discharged when the gage is set wrong." Let us state here that Tom did this, and never had another accident.

"Well, does this end the test?" asked Ned.

"No, indeed. I want you to try it, while I look on," spoke Tom. "We haven't any more stuffed figures to fire at, but I'll set up some targets. Come on, try your luck at a shot."

"I'm afraid I might disturb Mr. Moker, or some of the neighbors."

"No danger. I've got it adjusted right now. Come on, see if you can shatter this steel target," and Tom set up a small one at the end of the range.

Then, having properly fixed the weapon, Tom handed it to his chum, and, taking his place in a protected part of the gallery, prepared to watch the effect of the shot.

"Let her go!" cried Tom, and Ned pressed the button.

The effect was wonderful. Though there was no noise, smoke nor flame, the steel plate seemed to crumple up, and collapse as if it had been melted in the fire. There was a jagged hole through the center, but some frail boards back of it were not even splintered.

"Good shot!" cried Tom enthusiastically. "I had the distance gage right that time."

"You sure did," agreed Ned. "The electric bullet stopped as soon as it did its work on the plate. What's next?"

"I'm going to try a difficult test," explained Tom. "You know I said the gun would shoot luminous charges?"

"Yes."

"Well, I'm going to try that, now. I wish we had another image to shoot at, but I'll take a big dry-goods box, and make believe it's an elephant. Now, this is going to be a hard test, such as we'd meet with, if we were hunting in Africa. I want you to help me."

"What am I to do?" asked Ned.

"I want you to go outside," explained Tom, "set up a dry-goods box against the side of the little hill back of the shed, and not tell me where you put it. Then I'll go out, and, by means of the luminous charge, I'll locate the box, set the distance gage, and destroy it."

"Well, you can see it anyhow, in the moonlight," objected Ned.

"No, the moon is under a cloud now," explained Tom, looking out of a window. "It's quite dark, and will give me just the test I want for my new electric rifle."

"But won't it be dangerous, firing in the dark? Suppose you misjudge the distance, and the bullet, or charge, files off and hits some one?"

"It can't. I'll set the distance gage before I shoot. But if I should happen to make a mistake the charge will go into the side of the hill, and spend itself there. There is no danger. Go ahead, and set up the box, and then come and tell me. Mr. Jackson will help you."

Ned and the engineer left the gallery. As Tom had said, it was very dark now, and if Tom could see in the night to hit a box some distance away, his weapon would be all that he claimed for it.

"This will do," said the engineer, as he pointed to a box, one of several piled up outside the shed. The two could hardly see to make their way along, carrying it to the foot of the hill, and they stumbled several times. But at last it was in position, and then Ned departed to call Tom, and have him try the difficult test—that of hitting an object in the dark.

CHAPTER IV

BIG TUSKS WANTED

"Well, are you all ready for me?" asked the young inventor, as he took up his curious weapon, and followed Ned out into the yard. It was so dark that they had fairly to stumble along.

"Yes, we're ready," answered Ned. "And you'll be a good one, Tom, if you do this stunt. Now stand here" he went on, as he indicated a place as well as he could in the dark. "The box is somewhere in that direction," and he waved his hand vaguely. "I'm not going to tell you any more, and let's see you find it."

"Oh, I will, all right—or, rather, my electric rifle will," asserted Tom.

The inventor of the curious and terrible weapon took his position. Behind him stood Ned and Mr. Jackson, and just before Tom was ready to fire, his father came stalking through the darkness, calling to them.

"Are you there, Tom?"

"Yes Dad, is anything the matter?"

"No, but I thought I'd like to see what luck you have. Rad was saying you were going to have a test in the dark."

"I'm about ready for it," replied Tom. "I'm going to blow up a box that I can't see. You know how it's done, Dad, for you helped me in perfecting the luminous charge, but it's going to be something of a novelty to the others. Here we go, now!"

Tom raised his rifle, and aimed it in the dark. Ned Newton, straining his eyes to see, was sure the young inventor was pointing the gun at least twenty feet to one side of where the box was located, but he said nothing, for from experiences in the past, he realized that Tom knew what he was doing.

There was a little clicking sound, as the youth moved some gear wheel on his gun. Then there came a faint crackling noise, like some distant wireless apparatus beginning to flash a message through space.

Suddenly a little ball of purplish light shot through the darkness and sped forward like some miniature meteor. It shed a curious illuminating glow all about, and the ground, and the objects on it were brought into relief as by a lightning flash.

An instant later the light increased in intensity, and seemed to burst like some piece of aerial fireworks. There was a bright glare, in which Ned and the others could see the various buildings about the shed. They could see each other's faces, and they looked pale and ghastly in the queer glow. They could see the box, brought into bold relief, where Ned and the engineer had placed it.

Then, before the light had died away, they witnessed a curious sight. The heavy wooden box seemed to dissolve, to collapse and to crumple up like one of paper, and ere the last rays of the illuminating bullet faded, the watchers saw the splinters of wood fall back with a clatter in a little heap on the spot where the dry-goods case had been.

A silence followed, and the darkness was all the blacker by contrast with the intense light. At length Tom spoke, and he could not keep from his voice a note of triumph.

"Well, did I do it?" he asked.

"You sure did!" exclaimed Ned heartily.

"Fine!" cried Mr. Swift.

"Golly! I wouldn't gib much fo' de hide ob any burglar what comed around heah!" muttered Eradicate Sampson. "Dat box am knocked clean into nuffiness, Massa Tom."

"That's what I wanted to do," explained the lad. "And I guess this will end the test for tonight."

"But I don't exactly understand it," spoke Ned, as they all moved toward the Swift home, Eradicate going to the stable to see how his mule was. "Do you have two kinds of bullets, Tom, one for night and one for the daytime?"

"No," answered Tom, "there is only one kind of bullet, and, as I have said, that isn't a bullet at all. That is, you can't see it, or handle it, but you can feel it. Strictly speaking, it is a concentrated discharge of wireless electricity directed against a certain object. You can't see it any more than you can see a lightning bolt, though that is sometimes visible as a ball of fire. My electric rifle bullets are similar to a discharge of lightning, except that they are invisible."

"But we saw the one just now," objected Ned.

"No, you didn't see the bullet," said Tom.

"You saw the illuminating flash which I send out just before I fire, to reveal the object I am to hit. That is another part of my rifle and is only used at night."

"You see I shoot out a ball of electrical fire which will disclose the target, or the enemy at whom I am firing. As soon as that is discharged the rifle automatically gets ready to shoot the electric charge, and I have only to press the proper button, and the 'bullet,' as I call it, follows on the heels of the ball of light. Do you see?"

"Perfectly," exclaimed Ned with a laugh. "What a gun that would be for hunting, since most all wild beasts come out only at night."

"That was one object in making this invention," said Tom. "I only hope I get a chance to use it now."

"I thought you were going to Africa after elephants," spoke Mr. Swift.

“Well, I did think of it,” admitted Tom, “but I haven’t made any definite plans. But come into the house, Ned, and I’ll show you more in detail how my rifle works.”

Thereupon the two chums spent some time going into the mysteries of the new weapon. Mr. Swift and Mr. Jackson were also much interested, for, though they had seen the gun previously and had helped Tom perfect it, they had not yet tired of discussing its merits.

Ned stayed quite late that night, and promised to come over the next day, and watch Tom do some more shooting.

“I’ll show you how to use it, too,” promised the young inventor, and he was as good as his word, initiating Ned into the mysteries of the electric rifle, and showing him to store the charges of death- dealing electricity in the queer-looking stock.

For a week after that Tom and Ned practiced with the terrible gun, taking care not to have any more mishaps like the one that had marked the first night. They were both good shots with ordinary weapons and it was not long before they had equaled their record with the new instrument.

It was one warm afternoon, when Tom was out in the meadow at one side of his house, practicing with his rifle on some big boxes he had set up for targets, that he saw an elderly man standing close to the fence watching him. When Tom blew to pieces a particularly large packing-case, standing a long distance away from it, the stranger called to the youth.

“I beg your pardon,” he said, “but is that a dynamite gun you are using?”

“No, it’s an electric rifle,” was the answer.

“Would you mind telling me something about it?” went on the elderly man, and as Tom’s weapon was now fully protected by patents, the young inventor cordially invited the stranger to come nearer and see how it worked.

“That’s the greatest thing I ever saw!” exclaimed the man enthusiastically when Tom had blown up another box, and had told of the illumination for night firing. “The most wonderful weapon I ever heard of! What a gun it would be in my business.”

“What is your trade?” asked Tom curiously, for he had noted that the man, while aged, was rugged and hearty, and his skin was tanned a leathery brown, showing that he was much in the open air.

“I’m a hunter,” was the reply, “a hunter of big game, principally elephants, hippos and rhinoceroses. I’ve just finished a season in Africa, and I’m going back there again soon. I came on to New York to get a new elephant gun. I’ve got a sister living over in Waterford, and I’ve been visiting her. I went out for a stroll to- day, and I came farther than I intended. That’s how I happened to be passing here.”

“A sister in Waterford, eh?” mused Tom, wondering whether the elephant hunter had met Mr. Damon. “And how soon are you going hack to Africa, Mr.—er—” and Tom hesitated.

"Durban is my name, Alexander Durban," said the old man. "Why, I am to start back in a few weeks. I've got an order for a pair of big elephant tusks—the largest I can get for a wealthy New York man,— and I'm anxious to fulfil the contract. The game isn't what it once was. There's more competition and the elephants are scarcer. So I've got to hustle."

"I got me a new gun. But my! it's nothing to what yours is. With that weapon I could do about as I pleased. I could do night hunting, which is hard in the African jungle. Then I wouldn't have any trouble getting the big tusks I'm after. I could get a pair of them, and live easy the rest of my life. Yes, I wouldn't ask anything better than a gun like yours. But I s'pose they cost like the mischief?" He looked a question at Tom.

"This is the only one there is," was the lad's answer. "But I am very glad to have met you, Mr. Durban. Won't you come into the house? I'm sure my father will be glad to see you, and I have something I'd like to talk to you about," and Tom, with many wild ideas in his head, led the old elephant hunter toward the house.

The dream of the young inventor might come true after all.

CHAPTER V

RUSH WORK

Mr. Swift made the African hunter warmly welcome, and listened with pride to the words of praise Mr. Durban bestowed on Tom regarding the rifle.

"Yes, my boy has certainly done wonders along the inventive line," said Mr. Swift.

"Not half as much as you have, Dad," interrupted the lad, for Tom was a modest youth.

"You should see his sky racer," went on the old inventor.

"Sky racer? What's that?" asked Mr. Durban. "Is it another kind of gun or cannon?"

"It's an aeroplane—an airship," explained Mr. Swift.

"An airship!" exclaimed the old elephant hunter. "Say, you don't mean that you make balloons, do you?"

"Well, they're not exactly balloons," replied Tom, as he briefly explained what an aeroplane was, for Mr. Durban, having been in the wilds of the jungle so much, had had very little chance to see the wonders and progress of civilization.

"They are better than balloons," went on Tom, "for they can go where you want them to."

"Say! That's the very thing!" cried the old hunter enthusiastically. "If there's one thing more than another that is needed in hunting in Africa it's an airship. The travel through the jungle is something fierce, and that, more than anything else, interferes with my work. I can't cover ground enough, and when I do get on the track of a herd of elephants, and they get away, it's sometimes a week before I can catch up to them again."

"For, in spite of their size, elephants can travel very fast, and once they get on the go, nothing can stop them. An airship would be the very thing to hunt elephants with in Africa—an airship and this electric rifle. I wonder why you haven't thought of going, Tom Swift."

"I have thought of it," answered the young inventor, "and that's why I asked you in. I want to talk about it."

"Do you mean you want to go?" demanded the old man eagerly.

"I certainly do!"

"Then I'm your man! Say, Tom Swift, I'd be proud to have you go to Africa with me. I'd be proud to have you a member of my hunting party, and, though I don't like to boast, still if you'll ask any of the big-game people they'll tell you that not every one can accompany Aleck Durban."

Tom realized that he was speaking to an authority and a most desirable companion, should he go to Africa, and he was very glad of the chance that had made him acquainted with the veteran hunter.

"Will you go with me?" asked Mr. Durban. "You and your electric gun and your airship? Will you come to Africa to hunt elephants, and help me get the big tusks I'm after?"

"I will!" exclaimed Tom.

"Then we'll start at once. There's no need of delaying here any longer."

"Oh, but I haven't an airship ready," said the young inventor. The face of the old hunter expressed his disappointment.

"Then we'll have to give up the scheme," he said ruefully.

"Not at all," Tom told him. "I have all the material on hand for building a new airship. I have had it in mind for some time, and I have done some work on it. I stopped it to perfect my electric rifle, but, now that is done, I'll tackle the Black Hawk again, and rush that to completion."-

"The Black Hawk?" repeated Mr. Durban, wonderingly.

"Yes, that's what I will name my new craft. The RED CLOUD was destroyed, and so I thought I'd change the color this time, and avoid bad luck."

"Good!" exclaimed the hunter. "When do you think you can have it finished?"

"Oh, possibly in a month—perhaps sooner, and then we will go to Africa and hunt elephants!"

"Bless my ivory paper cutter!" exclaimed a voice in the hall just outside the library. "Bless my fingernails! But who's talking about going to Africa?"

The old hunter looked at Tom and his father in surprise, but the young inventor laughing and going to the door, called out:

"Come on in, Mr. Damon. I didn't hear you ring. There is some one here from your town."

"Is it my wife?" asked the odd gentleman who was always blessing something. "She said she was going to her mother's to spend a few weeks, and so I thought I'd come over here and see if you had anything new on the program. The first thing I hear is that you are going to Africa. And so there's some one from Waterford in there, eh? Is it my wife?"

"No," answered Tom with another laugh. "Come on in Mr. Damon."

"Bless my toothpick!" exclaimed the odd gentleman, as he saw the grizzled elephant hunter sitting between Tom and Mr. Swift. "I have seen you somewhere before, my dear sir."

"Yes," admitted Mr. Durban, "if you're from Waterford you have probably seen me traveling about the streets there. I'm stopping with my sister, Mrs. Douglass, but I can't stand it to be in the house much, so I'm out of doors, wandering about a good bit of the time. I miss my jungle. But we'll soon be in Africa, Tom Swift and me."

"Is it possible, Tom?" asked Mr. Damon. "Bless my diamond mines! but what are you going to do next?"

"It's hard to say," was the answer. "But you came just in time. Mr. Damon. I'm going to rush work on the Black Hawk, my newest airship, and we'll leave for elephant land inside of a month, taking my new electric rifle along. Will you come?"

"Bless my penknife! I never thought of such a thing. I—I—guess— no, I don't know about it—yes, I'll go!" he suddenly exclaimed. "I'll go! Hurrah for the elephants!" and he jumped up and shook hands in turn with Mr. Durban, to whom he had been formally introduced, and with Tom and Mr. Swift.

"Then it's all settled but the details," declared the youth, "and now I'll call in Mr. Jackson, and we'll talk about how soon we can have the airship ready."

"My, but you folks are almost as speedy as a herd of the big elephants themselves!" exclaimed Mr. Durban, and with the advent of the engineer the talk turned to things mechanical among Tom and Mr. Jackson and Mr. Damon, while Mr. Durban told Mr. Swift hunting stories which the old inventor greatly enjoyed.

The next day Tom engaged two machinists who had worked for him building airships before, and in the next week rush work began on the new Black Hawk. Meanwhile Mr. Durban was a frequent visitor at Tom's home, where he learned to use the new rifle, declaring it was even more wonderful than he had at first supposed.

"That will get the elephants!" he exclaimed. It did, as you shall soon learn, and it also was the means of saving several lives in the wilds of the African jungle.

CHAPTER VI

NEWS FROM ANDY

Tom Swift's former airship, the Red Cloud, had been such a fine craft, and had done such good service that he thought, in building a successor, that he could do no better than to follow the design of the skyship which had been destroyed in the ice caves. But, on talking with the old elephant hunter, and learning something of the peculiarities of the African jungle the young inventor decided on certain changes.

In general the Black Hawk would be on the lines of the Red Cloud but it would be smaller and lighter and would also be capable of swifter motion.

"You want it so that it will rise and descend quickly and at sharp angles," said Mr. Durban.

"Why," inquired Tom.

"Because in Africa, at least in the part where we will go, there are wide patches of jungle and forest, with here and there big open places. If you are skimming along close to the ground, in an open place, in pursuit of a herd of elephants and they should suddenly plunge into the forest, you would want to be able to rise above the trees quickly."

"That's so," admitted Tom. "Then I'll have to use a smaller gas bag than we had on the other ship, for the air resistance to that big one made us go slowly at times."

"Will it be as safe with a small bag?" Mr. Damon wanted to know.

"Yes, for I will use a more powerful gas, so that we will be more quickly lifted," said the young inventor. "I will also retain the aeroplane feature, so that the Black Hawk will be a combined biplane and dirigible balloon. But it will have many new features. I have the plans all drawn for a new style of gas generating apparatus, and I think it can be made in time."

There were busy days about the Swift home. Mrs. Baggert, the housekeeper, was in despair. She said the good meals she got ready were wasted, because no one would come to table when they were ready. She would ring the bell, and announce that dinner would be served in five minutes.

Then Tom would shout from his workshop that he could not leave until he had inserted a certain lever in place. Mr. Jackson would positively decline to sit down until he had screwed fast some part of a machine. Even Mr. Swift, who, because of his recent illness, was not allowed to do much, would often delay his meal to test some new style of gears.

As for Mr. Damon, it was to be expected that he would be eccentric as he always was. He was not an expert mechanic, but he knew something of machinery and was of considerable help to Tom in the rush work on the airship. He would hear the dinner bell ring, and would exclaim:

"Bless my napkin ring! I can't come now. I have to fix up this electrical register first."

And so it would go. Eradicate and Boomerang, his mule, were the only ones who ate regularly, and they always insisted on stopping at exactly twelve o'clock to partake of the noonday meal.

"'Cause ef I didn't," explained the colored man, "dat contrary mule ob mine would lay down in de dust ob de road an' not move a step, lessen' he got his oats. So dat's why we has t' eat, him an' me."

"Well, I'm glad there's some one who's got sense," murmured Mrs. Baggert. Eradicate and Boomerang were of great service in the hurried work that followed, for the colored man in his cart brought from town, or from the freight depot, many things that Tom needed.

The young inventor was very enthusiastic about his proposed trip, and at night, after a hard day's work in the shop, he would read books on African hunting, or he would sit and listen to the stories told by Mr. Durban. And the latter knew how to tell hunting tales, for he had been long in his dangerous calling, and had had many narrow escapes.
"And there are other dangers than from elephants and wild beasts in Africa," he said.
"Bless my toothbrush!" exclaimed Mr. Damon. "Do you mean cannibals, Mr. Durban?"
"Some cannibals," was the reply. "But they're not the worst. I mean the red pygmies. I hope we don't get into their clutches."
"Red pygmies!" repeated Tom, wonderingly.
"Yes, they're a tribe of little creatures, about three feet high, covered with thick reddish hair, who live in the central part of Africa, near some of the best elephant-hunting ground. They are wild, savage and ferocious, and what they lack individually in strength, they make up in numbers. They're like little red apes, and woe betide the unlucky hunter who falls into their merciless hands. They treat him worse than the cannibals do."
"Then we'll look out for them," said Tom. "But I fancy my electric rifle will make them give us a wide berth."
"It's a great gun," admitted the old hunter with a shake of his head, "but those red pygmies are terrible creatures. I hope we don't get them on our trail. But tell me, Tom, how are you coming on with the airship? for I don't know much about mechanics, and to me it looks as if it would never be put together. It's like one of those queer puzzles I've seen 'em selling in the streets of London."
"Oh, it's nearer ready than it looks to be," said Tom. "We'll have it assembled, and ready for a trial in about two weeks more."
Work on the Black Hawk was rushed more than ever in the next few days, another extra machinist being engaged. Then the craft began to assume shape and form, and with the gas bag partly inflated and the big planes stretching out from either side, it began to look something like the ill-fated Red Cloud.
"It's going to be a fine ship!" cried Tom enthusiastically, one day, as he went to the far side of the ship to get a perspective view of it. "We'll make good time in this."
"Are you going to sail all the way to Africa—across the ocean—in her?" asked Mr. Durban, in somewhat apprehensive tones.

"Oh, no," replied Tom. "I believe she would be capable of taking us across the ocean, but there is no need of running any unnecessary risks. I want to get her safely to Africa, and have her do stunts in elephant land."
"Then what are your plans?" asked the hunter.
"We'll put her together here," said Tom, "give her a good try-out to see that she works well, and then pack her up for shipment to the African coast by steamer. We'll go on the same ship, and when we arrive we'll put the Black Hawk together again, and set sail for the interior."
"Good idea," commented Mr. Durban. "Now, if you've no objections, I'm going to do a little practice with the electric rifle."
"Go ahead," assented Tom. "There comes Ned Newton; he'll be glad of a chance for a few shots while I work on this new propeller motor. It just doesn't suit me."
The bank clerk, who had arranged to go to Africa with Tom, was seen advancing toward the aeroplane shed. In his hand Ned held a paper, and as he saw Tom he called out:
"Have you heard the news?"
"What news?" inquired the young inventor.
"About Andy Foger. He and his aeroplane are lost!"
"Lost!" cried Tom, for in spite of the mean way the bully had treated him our hero did not wish him any harm.
"Well, not exactly lost," went on Ned, as he held out the paper to Tom, "but he and his sky-craft have disappeared."
"Disappeared?"
"Yes. You know he and that German, Mr. Landbacher, went over to Europe to give some aviation exhibitions. Well, I see by this paper that they went to Egypt, and were doing a high-flying stunt there, when a gale sprang up, they lost control of the aeroplane and it was swept out of sight."

"In which direction; out to sea?"

"No, toward the interior of Africa."

"Toward the interior of Africa!" cried Tom. "And that's where we're going in a couple of weeks. Andy in Africa!"

"'Maybe we'll see him there," suggested Ned.

"Well, I certainly hope we do not!" exclaimed Tom, as he turned back to his work, with an undefinable sense of fear in his heart.

CHAPTER VII

THE BLACK HAWK FLIES

It was with no little surprise that the news of the plight that was said to have befallen Andy Foger was received by Tom and his associates. The newspaper had quite an account of the affair, and, even allowing the usual discount for the press dispatches, it looked as if the former bully was in rather distressing circumstances.

"He won't have to be carried very far into Africa to be in a bad country," said the old hunter. "Of course, some parts of the continent are all right, and for me, I like it all, where there's hunting to be had. But I guess your young friend Foger won't care for it."

"He's no friend of ours," declared Ned, as Tom was reading the newspaper account. "Still, I don't wish him any bad luck, and I do hope he doesn't become the captive of the red pygmies."

"So do I," echoed the old hunter fervently. There was no news of Andy in the papers the next day, though there were cable dispatches speculating on what might have happened to him and the airship. In Shopton the dispatches created no little comment, and it was said that Mr. Foger was going to start for Africa at once to rescue his son. This, however, could not be confirmed.

Meanwhile Tom and his friends were very busy over the Black Hawk. Every hour saw the craft nearer completion, for the young inventor had had much experience in this sort of work now, and knew just how to proceed.

To Mr. Damon were intrusted certain things which he could well attend to, and though he frequently stopped to bless his necktie or his shoelaces, still he got along fairly well.

There would be no necessity of purchasing supplies in this country, for they could get all they needed in the African city of Majumba, on the western coast, where they planned to land. There the airship would be put together, stocked with provisions and supplies, and they would begin their journey inland. They planned to head for Buka Meala, crossing the Congo River, and then go into the very interior of the heart of the dark continent.

As we have described in detail, in the former books of this series, the construction of Tom Swift's airship, the Red Cloud, and as the Black Hawk was made in a similar manner to that, we will devote but brief space to it now. As the story proceeds, and the need arises for a description of certain features, we will give them to you, so that you will have a clear idea of what a wonderful craft it was.

Sufficient to say that there was a gas bag, made of a light but strong material, and capable of holding enough vapor, of a new and secret composition, to lift the airship with its load. This was the dirigible-balloon feature of the craft, and with the two powerful propellers, fore and aft (in which particular the Black Hawk differed from the Red Cloud which had two forward propellers);—with these two powerful wooden screws, as we have said, the new ship could travel swiftly without depending on the wing planes.

But as there is always a possibility of the gas bag being punctured, or the vapor suddenly escaping from one cause or another, Tom did not depend on this alone to keep his craft afloat. It was a perfect aeroplane, and with the gas bag entirely empty could be sent scudding along at any height desired. To enable it to rise by means of the wings, however, it was necessary to start it in motion along the ground, and for this purpose wheels were provided.

There was a large body or car to the craft, suspended from beneath the gas bag, and in this car were the cabins, the living, sleeping and eating apartments, the storerooms and the engine compartment.

This last was a marvel of skill, for it contained besides the gas machine, and the motor for working the propellers, dynamos, gages, and instruments for telling the speed and height, motors for doing various pieces of work, levers, wheels, cogs, gears, tanks for storing the lifting gas, and other features of interest.

There were several staterooms for the use of the young captain and the passengers, an observation and steering tower, a living-room, where they could all assemble as the ship was sailing through the air, and a completely equipped kitchen.

This last was Mr. Damon's special pride, as he was a sort of cook, and he liked nothing better than to get up a meal when the craft was two or three miles high, and scudding along at seventy-five miles an hour.

In addition there were to be taken along many scientific instruments, weapons of defense and offense, in addition to the electric rifle, and various other objects which will be spoken of in due time.

"Well," remarked Tom Swift one afternoon, following a hard day's work in the shop, "I think, if all goes well, and we have good weather, I'll give the Black Hawk a trial tomorrow."

"Do you think it will fly?" asked Ned.

"There is no telling," was the answer of the young inventor. "These things are more or less guesswork, even when you make two exactly alike. As far as I can tell, we have now a better craft than the Red Cloud was, but it remains to be seen how she will behave."

They worked late that night, putting the finishing touches on the Black Hawk, and in the morning the new airship was wheeled out of the shed, and placed on the level starting ground, ready for the trial flight.

Only the bare machinery was in her, as yet, and the gas bag had not been inflated as Tom wanted to try the plane feature first. But the vapor machine was all ready to start generating the gas whenever it was needed. Nor was the Black Hawk painted and decorated as she would be when ready to be sent to Africa. On the whole, she looked rather crude as she rested there on the bicycle wheels, awaiting the starting of the big propellers. As the stores and supplies were not yet in, Tom took aboard, in addition to Mr. Damon, Ned, his father, Mr.

Jackson and Mr. Durban, some bags of sand to represent the extra weight that would have to be carried.

"If she'll rise with this load she'll do," announced the young inventor, as he went carefully over the craft, looking to see that everything was in shape.

"If she does rise it will be a new experience for me," spoke the old elephant hunter. "I've never been in an airship before. It doesn't seem possible that we can get up in the air with this machine."

"Maybe we won't," spoke Tom, who was always a little diffident about a new piece of machinery.

"Well, if it doesn't do it the first time, it will the second, or the fifty-second," declared Ned Newton. "Tom Swift doesn't give up until he succeeds."

"Stop it! You'll make me blush!" cried the Black Hawk's owner as he tried the different gages and levers to see that they were all right.

After what seemed like a long time he gave the word for those who were to make the trial trip to take their places. They did so, and then, with Mr. Jackson, Tom went to the engine room. There was a little delay, due to the fact that some adjustment was necessary on the main motor. But at last it was fixed.

"Are you all ready?" called Tom.

"All ready," answered Mr. Damon. The old elephant hunter sat in a chair, nervously gripping the arms, and with a grim look on his tanned face. Mr. Swift was cool, as Ned, for they had made many trips in the air. Outside were Eradicate Sampson and Mrs. Baggert.

"Here we go!" suddenly cried Tom, and he yanked over the lever that started the main motor and propellers. The Black Hawk trembled throughout her entire length. She shivered and shook. Faster and faster whirled the great wooden screws. The motor hummed and throbbed.

Slowly the Black Hawk moved across the ground. Then she gathered speed. Now she was fairly rushing over the level space. Tom Swift tilted the elevation rudder, and with a suddenness that was startling, at least to the old elephant hunter, the new airship shot upward on a steep slant.

"The Black Hawk flies!" yelled Ned Newton. "Now for elephant land and the big tusks!"

"Yes, and perhaps for the red pygmies, too," added Tom in a low voice. Then he gave his whole attention to the management of his new machine, which was rapidly mounting upward, with a speed rivalling that of his former big craft.

CHAPTER VIII

OFF FOR AFRICA

Higher and higher went the Black Hawk, far above the earth, until the old elephant hunter, looking down, said in a voice which he tried to make calm and collected, but which trembled in spite of himself:

"Of course I'm not an expert at this game, Tom Swift, but it looks to me as if we'd never get down. Don't you think we're high enough?"

"For the time being, yes," answered the young inventor. "I didn't think she'd climb so far without the use of the gas. She's doing well."

"Bless my topknot, yes!" exclaimed Mr. Damon. "She beats the Red Cloud, Tom. Try her on a straight-away course."

Which the youth did, pointing the nose of the craft along parallel to the surface of the earth, and nearly a mile above it. Then, increasing the speed of the motor, and with the big propellers humming, they made fast time.

The old elephant hunter grew more calm as he saw that the airship did not show any inclination to fall, and he noted that Tom and the others not only knew how to manage it, but took their flight as much a matter of course as if they were in an automobile skimming along on the surface of the ground.

Tom put his craft through a number of evolutions, and when he found that she was in perfect control as an aeroplane, he started the gas machine, filled the big black bag overhead, and, when it was sufficiently buoyant, he shut off the motor, and the Black Hawk floated along like a balloon.

"That's what we'll do if our power happens to give out when we get over an African jungle, with a whole lot of wild elephants down below, and a forest full of the red pygmies waiting for us," explained Tom to Mr. Durban.

"And I guess you'll need to do it, too," answered the hunter. "I don't know which I fear worse, the bad elephants wild with rage, as they get some times, or the little red men who are as strong as gorillas, and as savage as wolves. It would be all up with us if we got into their hands. But I think this airship will be just what we need in Africa. I'd have been able to get out of many a tight place if I had had one on my last trip."

While the Black Hawk hung thus, up the air, not moving, save as the wind blew her, Tom with his father and Mr. Jackson made an inspection of the machinery to find out whether it had been strained any. They found that it had worked perfectly, and soon the craft was in motion again, her nose this time being pointed toward the earth. Tom let out some of the gas, and soon the airship was on the ground in front of the shed she had so recently left.

"She's all right," decided the young inventor after a careful inspection. "I'll give her a couple more trials, put on the finishing touches and then we'll be ready for our trip to Africa. Have you got everything arranged to go, Ned?"

"Sure. I have a leave of absence from the bank, thanks to your father and Mr. Damon, most of my clothes are packed, I've bought a gun and I've got a lot of quinine in case I get a fever."

"Good!" cried the elephant hunter. "You'll do all right, I reckon. I'm glad I met you young fellows. Well, I've lived through my first trip in the air, which is more than I expected when I started."

They discussed their plans at some length, for, now that the airship had proved all that they had hoped for, it would not be long ere they were under way. In the days that followed Tom put the finishing touches on the craft, arranged to have it packed up for shipment, and spent some time practicing with his electric rifle. He got to be an expert shot, and Mr. Durban, who was a wonder with the ordinary rifle, praised the young inventor highly.

"There won't be many of the big tuskers get away from you, Tom Swift," he said. "And that reminds me, I got a letter the other day, from the firm I collect ivory for, stating that the price had risen because of a scarcity, and urging me to hurry back to Africa and get all I could. It seems that war has broken out among some of the central African tribes, and they are journeying about in the jungle, on the war path here and there, and have driven the elephants into the very deepest wilds, where the ordinary hunters can't get at them."

"Maybe we won't have any luck, either," suggested Ned.

"Oh, yes, we will," declared the hunter. "With our airship, the worst forest of the dark continent won't have any terrors for us, for we can float above it. And the fights of the natives won't have any effect. In a way, this will be a good thing, for with the price of ivory soaring, we can make more money than otherwise. There's a chance for us all to get a lot of money."

"Bless my piano keys!" exclaimed Mr. Damon, "if I can get just one elephant, and pull out his big ivory teeth, I'll be satisfied. I want a nice pair of tusks to set up on either side of my fireplace for ornaments."

"A mighty queer place for such-like ornaments," said Mr. Durban in a low voice. Then he added: "Well, the sooner we get started the better I'll like it, for I want to get that pair of big tusks for a special customer of mine."

"I'll give the Black Hawk one more trial flight, and then take her apart and ship her," decided Tom, and the final flight, a most successful one, took place the following day.

Then came another busy season when the airship was taken apart for shipment to the coast of Africa by steamer. It was put into big boxes and crates, and Eradicate and his mule took them to the station in Shopton.

"Don't you want to come to Africa with us, Rad?" asked Tom, when the last of the cases had been sent off. "You'll find a lot of your friends there."

"No, indeedy, I doan't want t' go," answered the colored man, "though I would like to see dat country."

"Then why don't you come?"

"Hu! Yo' think, Massa Tom, dat I go anywhere dat I might meet dem little red men what Massa Durban talk about? No, sah, dey might hurt mah mule Boomerang."

"Oh, I wasn't going to take the mule along," said Tom, wondering how the creature might behave in the airship.

"Not take Boomerang? Den I SUTTINLY ain't goin," and Eradicate walked off, highly offended, to give some oats to his faithful if somewhat eccentric steed.

After the airship had been sent off there yet remained much for Tom Swift to do. He had to send along a number of special tools and appliances with which to put the ship together again, and also some with which to repair the craft in case of accident. So that this time was pretty well occupied. But at length everything was in readiness, and with his electric rifle knocked down for transportation, and with his baggage, and that of the others, all packed, they set off one morning to take the train for New York, where they would get a steamer for Africa.

Numerous good-bys had been said, and Tom had made a farewell call on Mary Nestor, promising to bring her some trophy from elephant land, though he did not quite know what it would be.

Mr. Damon, as the train started, blessed everything he could think of. Mr. Swift waved his hand and wished his son and the others good luck, feeling a little lonesome that he could not make one of the party. Ned was eager with excitement, and anticipation of what lay before him. Tom Swift was thinking of what he could accomplish with his electric rifle, and of the wonderful sights he would see, and, as for the old elephant hunter, he was very glad to be on the move again, after so many weeks of idleness, for he was a very active man.

Their journey to New York was uneventful, and they found that the parts of the airship had safely arrived, and had been taken aboard the steamer. The little party went aboard themselves, after a day spent in sight-seeing, and that afternoon the Soudalar, which was the vessel's name, steamed away from the dock at high tide.

"Off for Africa!" exclaimed Tom to Ned, as they stood at the rail, watching the usual crowd wave farewells. "Off for Africa, Ned."

As Tom spoke, a gentleman who had been standing near him and his chum, vigorously waving his hand to some one on the pier, turned quickly. He looked sharply at the young inventor for a moment, and then exclaimed:

"Well, if it isn't Tom Swift! Did I hear you say you were going to Africa?"

Tom looked at the gentleman with rather a puzzled air for a moment. The face was vaguely familiar, but Tom could not recall where he had seen it. Then it came to him in a flash.

"Mr. Floyd Anderson!" exclaimed our hero. "Mr. Anderson of—"

"Earthquake Island!" exclaimed the gentleman quickly, as he extended his hand. "I guess you remember that place, Tom Swift."

"Indeed I do. And to think of meeting you again, and on this African steamer," and Tom's mind went back to the perilous days when his wireless message had saved the castaways of Earthquake Island, among whom were Mr. Anderson and his wife.

"Did I hear you say you were going to Africa?" asked Mr. Anderson, when he had been introduced to Ned, and the others in Tom's party.

"That's where we're bound for," answered the lad. "We are going to elephant land. But where are you going, Mr. Anderson?"

"Also to Africa, but not on a trip for pleasure or profit like yourselves. I have been commissioned by a missionary society to rescue two of its workers from the heart of the dark continent."

"Rescue two missionaries?" exclaimed Tom, wonderingly.

"Yes, a gentleman and his wife, who, it is reported, have fallen into the hands of a race known as the red pygmies, who hold them captives!"

CHAPTER IX

ATTACKED BY A WHALE

Surprise at Mr. Anderson's announcement held Tom silent for a moment. That the gentleman whom he had been the means of rescuing, among others, from Earthquake Island, should be met with so unexpectedly, was quite a coincidence, but when it developed that he was bound to the same part of the African continent as were Tom and his friends, and when he said he hoped to rescue some missionaries from the very red pygmies so feared by the old elephant hunter—this was enough to startle any one.

"I see that my announcement has astonished you," said Mr. Anderson, as he noted the look of surprise on the face of the young inventor.

"It certainly has! Why, that's where we are bound for, in my new airship. Come down into our cabin, Mr. Anderson, and tell us all about it. Is your wife with you?"

"No, it is too dangerous a journey on which to take her. I have little hope of succeeding, for it is now some time since the unfortunate missionaries were captured, but I am going to do my best, and organize a relief expedition when I get to Africa."

Tom said nothing at that moment, but he made up his mind that if it was at all possible he would lend his aid, that of his airship, and also get his friends to assist Mr. Anderson. They went below to a special cabin that had been reserved for Tom's party, and there, as the ship slowly passed down New York Bay, Mr. Anderson told his story.

"I mentioned to you, when we were on Earthquake Island," he said to Tom, "that I had been in Africa, and had done some hunting. That is not my calling, as it is that of your friend, Mr. Durban, but I know the country pretty well. However, I have not been there in some time."

"My wife and I are connected with a church in New York that, several years ago, raised a fund and sent two missionaries, Mr. and Mrs. Jacob Illingway, to the heart of Africa. They built up a little mission there, and for a time all went well, and they did good work among the natives."

"They are established in a tribe of friendly black men, of simple nature, and, while the natives did not become Christianized to any remarkable extent, yet they were kind to the missionaries. Mr. and Mrs. Illingway used frequently to write to members of our church, telling of their work. They also mentioned the fact that adjoining the country of the friendly blacks there was a tribe of fierce little red men,—red because of hair of that color all over their bodies."

"That's right," agreed Mr. Durban, shaking his head solemnly. "They're red imps, too!"

"Mr. Illingway often mentioned in his letters," went on Mr. Anderson, "that there were frequent fights between the pygmies and the race of blacks, but the latter had no great fear of their small enemies. However, it seems that they did not take proper precautions, for not long ago there was a great battle, the blacks were attacked by a large force of the red pygmies, who overwhelmed them by numbers, and finally routed them, taking possession of their country."

"What became of the missionaries?" asked Ned Newton.

"I'll tell you," said Mr. Anderson. "For a long time we heard nothing, beyond the mere news of the fight, which we read of in the papers. The church people were very anxious about the fate of Mr. and Mrs. Illingway, and were talking of sending a special messenger to inquire about them, when a cablegram came from the headquarters of the society in London."

"It seems that one of the black natives, named Tomba, who was a sort of house servant to Mr. and Mrs. Illingway, escaped the general massacre, in which all his friends were killed. He made his way through the jungle to a white settlement, and told his story, relating how the two missionaries had been carried away captive by the pygmies."

"A terrible fate," commented Mr. Durban.

"Yes, they might better be dead, from all the accounts we can hear," went on Mr. Anderson.

"Bless my Sunday hat! Don't say that!" exclaimed Mr. Damon. "Maybe we can save them, Mr. Anderson."

"That is what I am going to try to do, though it may be too late. As soon as definite news was received, our church held a meeting, raised a fund, and decided to send me off to find Mr. and Mrs. Illingway, if alive, or give them decent burial, if I could locate their bones. The reason they selected me was because I had been in Africa, and knew the country."

"I made hurried arrangements, packed up, said good-by to my wife, and here I am. But to think of meeting you, Tom Swift! And to hear that you are also going to Africa. I wish I could command an airship for the rescue. It might be more easily accomplished!"

"That's just what I was going to propose!" exclaimed Tom. "We are going to the land of the red pygmies, and while I have promised to help Mr. Durban in getting ivory, and while I want to try my electric rifle on big game, still we can do both, I think. You can depend on us, Mr. Anderson, and if the Black Hawk can be of any service to you in the rescue, count us in!"

"Gosh!" cried the former castaway of Earthquake Island. "This is the best piece of luck I could have! Now tell me all about your plans." which Tom and the others did, listening in turn, to further details about the missionaries.

Just how they would go to work to effect the rescue, or how they could locate the particular tribe of little red men who had Mr. and Mrs. Illingway, they did not know.

"We may be able to get hold of this Tomba," said Mr. Durban. "If not I guess between Mr. Anderson and myself we can get on the trail, somehow. I'm anxious to get to the coast, see the airship put together again, and start for the interior."

"So am I," declared Tom, as he got out his electric rifle, and began to put it together, for he wanted to show Mr. Anderson how it worked.

They had a pleasant and uneventful voyage for two weeks. The weather was good, and, to tell the truth, it was rather monotonous for Tom and the others, who were eager to get into activity again. Then came a storm, which, while it was not dangerous, yet gave them plenty to think and talk about for three days. Then came more calm weather, when the Soudalar plowed along over gently heaving billows.

They were about a week from their port of destination, which was Majumba, on the African coast, when, one afternoon, as Tom and the others were in their cabin, they heard a series of shouts on deck, and the sound of many feet running to and fro.

"Something has happened!" exclaimed the young inventor.

Tom raced for the companionway, and was soon on deck, followed by Mr. Durban and the others. They saw a crowd of sailors and passengers leaning over the port rail.

"What's the matter?" asked Tom, of the second mate, who was just passing.

"Fight between a killer and a whale," was the reply. "The captain has ordered the ship to lay-to so it can be watched."

Tom made his way to the rail. About a quarter of a mile away there could be observed a great commotion in the ocean. Great bodies seemed to be threshing about, beating the water to foam, and, with the foam could be seen bright blood mingled. Occasionally two jets of water, as from some small fountain, would shoot upward.

"He's blowing hard!" exclaimed one of the sailors. "I guess he's about done for!"

"Which one?" asked Tom.

"The whale," was the reply. "The killer has the best of the big fellow," and the sailor quickly explained how the smaller killer fish, by the peculiarity of its attack, and its great ferocity, often bested its larger antagonist.

The battle was now at its height, and Tom and the others were interested spectators. At times neither of the big creatures could be seen, because of the smother of foam in which they rolled and threshed about. The whale endeavored to sound, or go to the bottom, but the killer stuck to him relentlessly.

Suddenly, however, as Tom looked, the whale, by a stroke of his broad tail, momentarily stunned his antagonist. Instantly realizing that he was free the great creature, which was about ninety feet long, darted away, swimming on the surface of the water, for he needed to get all the air possible.

Quickly acquiring momentum, the whale came on like a locomotive, spouting at intervals, the vapor from the blowholes looking not unlike steam from some submarine boat.

"He looks to be heading this way," remarked Mr. Durban to Tom.

"He is," agreed the young inventor, "but I guess he'll dive before he gets here. He only wants to get away from the killer. Look, the other one is swimming this way, too!"

“Bless my harpoon, but he sure is!” called Mr. Damon. “They’ll renew the fight near here.”

But he was mistaken, for the killer, after coming a little distance after the whale, suddenly turned, hesitated for a moment, and then disappeared in the depths of the ocean.

The whale, however, continued to come on, speeding through the water with powerful strokes. There was an uneasy movement among some of the passengers.

“Suppose he strikes the ship,” suggested one woman.

“Nonsense! He couldn’t,” said her husband.

“The old man had better get under way, just the same,” remarked a sailor near Tom, as he looked up at the bridge where the captain was standing.

The “old man,” or commander, evidently thought the same thing, for, after a glance at the oncoming leviathan, which was still headed directly for the vessel, he shoved the lever of the telegraph signal over to “full speed ahead.”

Hardly had he done so than the whale sank from sight.

“Oh, I’m so glad!” exclaimed the woman who had first spoken of the possibility of the whale hitting the ship, “I am afraid of those terrible creatures.”

“They’re as harmless as a cow, unless they get angry,” said her husband.

Slowly the great ship began to move through the water. Tom and his friends were about to go back to their cabin, for they thought the excitement over, when, as the young inventor turned from the rail, he felt a vibration throughout the whole length of the steamer, as if it had hit on a sand-bar.

Instantly there was a jangling of bells in the engine room, and the Soudalar lost headway.

“What’s the matter?” asked several persons.

They were answered a moment later, for the big whale, even though grievously wounded in his fight with the killer, had risen not a hundred feet away from the ship, and was coming toward it with the speed of an express train.

“Bless my blubber!” cried Mr. Damon. “We must have hit the whale, or it hit us under the water and now it’s going to attack us!”

He had no more than gotten the words out of his mouth ere the great creature of the deep came on full tilt at the vessel, struck it a terrific blow which made it tremble from stem to stern, and careen violently.

There was a chorus of frightened cries, sailors rushed to and fro, the engine-room bells rang violently, and the captain and mates shouted hoarse orders.

“Here he comes again!” yelled Mr. Durban, as he hurried to the side of the ship. “The whale takes us for an enemy, I guess, and he’s going to ram us again!”

“And if he does it many times, he’ll start the plates and cause a leak that won’t be stopped in a hurry!” cried a sailor as he rushed past Tom.

The young inventor looked at the oncoming monster for a moment, and then started on the run for his cabin.

“Here! Where are you going?” cried Mr. Damon, but Tom did not answer.

CHAPTER X

OFF IN THE AIRSHIP

As Tom Swift hurried down the companionway he again felt the ship careen as the whale struck it a powerful blow, and he was almost knocked off his feet. But he kept on.

Below he found some frightened men and women, a number of whom were adjusting life preservers about them, under the impression that the ship had struck a rock and was going down. They had not been up on deck, and did not know of the battle between the killer and the whale, nor what followed.

"Oh, I know we're sinking!" cried one timid woman. "What has happened?" she appealed to Tom.

"It will be all right in a little while," he assured her.

"But what is it? I want to know. Have we had a collision."

"Yes, with a whale," replied Tom, as he grabbed up something from his stateroom, and again rushed up on deck. As he reached it the whale came on once more, and struck the ship another terrific blow. Then the monster sank and could be seen swimming back, just under the surface of the water, getting ready to renew the attack.

"He's going to ram us again!" cried Mr. Damon. "Bless my machine oil! Why doesn't the captain do something?"

At that moment the commander cried from the bridge:

"Send a man below, Mr. Laster, to see if we are making any water. Then tell half a dozen of the sailors to get out the rifles, and see if they can't kill the beast. He'll put us in Davy Jones's locker if he keeps this up! Lively now, men!"

The first mate, Mr. Laster, called out the order. A sailor went below to see if the ship was leaking much, and the captain rang for full speed ahead. But the Soudalar was slow in getting under way again, and, even at top speed she was no match for the whale, which was again rushing toward the vessel.

"Quick with those rifles!" cried the captain. "Fire a volley into the beast!"

"There's no need!" suddenly called Mr. Damon, who had caught sight of Tom Swift, and the object which the lad carried.

"No need?" demanded the commander. "Why, has the whale sunk, or made off?"

"No," answered the eccentric man, "the whale is still coming on, but Tom Swift will fix him. Get there, Tom, and let him have a good one!"

"What sort of a gun is that?" demanded the commander as the young inventor took his place at the rail, which was now almost deserted.

Tom did not answer. Bracing himself against the rolling and heaving of the vessel, which was now under about half speed, Tom aimed his electric rifle at the oncoming leviathan. He looked at the automatic gage, noted the distance and waiting a moment until the crest of a wave in front of the whale had subsided, he pressed the button.

If those watching him expected to hear a loud report, and see a flash of flame, they were disappointed. There was absolutely no sound, but what happened to the whale was most surprising.

The great animal stopped short amid a swirl of foam, and the next instant it seemed to disintegrate. It went all to pieces, just as had the dummy figure which Tom on one occasion fired at with his rifle and as had the big packing-cases. The whale appeared to dissolve, as does a lump of sugar in a cup of hot tea, and, five seconds after Tom Swift had fired his electric gun, there was not a sign of the monster save a little blood on the calm sea.

"What—what happened?" asked the captain in bewilderment. "Is—is that monster gone?"

"Completely gone!" cried Mr. Damon. "Bless my powder horn, Tom, but I knew you could do it!"

"Is that a new kind of whale gun, firing an explosive bullet?" inquired the commander, as he came down off the bridge and shook hands with Tom. "If it is, I'd like to buy one. We may be rammed again by another whale."

"This is my new, electric rifle," explained the young inventor modestly, "and it fires wireless charges of electricity instead of bullets. I'm sorry I can't let you have it, as it's the only one I have. But I guess no more whales will ram us. That one was evidently crazed by the attack of the killer, and doubtless took us for another of its enemies."

Sailors and passengers crowded around Tom, eager to shake his hand, and to hear about the gun. Many declared that he had saved the ship.

This was hardly true, for the whale could not have kept up its attacks much longer. Still he might have done serious damage, by causing a leak, and, while the Soudalar was a stanch craft, with many water-tight compartments, still no captain likes to be a week from land with a bad leak, especially if a storm comes up. Then, too, there was the danger of a panic among the passengers, had the attacks been kept up, so, though Tom wanted to make light of his feat, the others would not let him.

"You're entitled to the thanks of all on board," declared Captain Wendon, "and I'll see that the owners hear of what you did. Well, I guess we can go on, now. I'll not stop again to see a fight between a killer and a whale."

The steamer resumed her way at full speed, and the sailor, who had gone below, came up to report that there was only a slight leak, which need not cause any uneasiness.

Little was talked of for the next few days but the killing of the whale, and Tom had to give several exhibitions of his electric rifle, and explain its workings. Then, too, the story of his expedition became known, and also the object of Mr. Anderson's quest, and Tom's offer of aid to help rescue the missionaries, so that, altogether, our hero was made much of during the remainder of the voyage.

"Well, if your gun will do that to a whale, what will it do to an elephant?" asked Mr. Durban one morning, when they were within a day's steaming of their port. "I'm afraid it's almost too strong, Tom. It will leave nothing—not even the tusks to pick up."

"Oh, I can regulate the power," declared the lad. "I used full force on the whale, just to see what it would do. It was the first time I'd tried it on anything alive. I can so regulate the charge that it will kill even an elephant, and leave scarcely a mark on the beast."

"I'd like to see it done," remarked the old hunter.

"I'll show you, if we sight any sharks," promised Tom. He was able to keep his word for that afternoon a school of the ugly fish followed the steamer for the sake of the food scraps thrown overboard. Tom took his position in the stern, and gave an exhibition of shooting with his electric gun that satisfied even Mr. Durban, exacting as he was.

For the lad, by using his heaviest charges, destroyed the largest sharks so that they seemed to instantly disappear in the water, and from that he toned down the current until he could kill some of the monsters so easily and quickly that they seemed to float motionless on the surface, yet there was no life left in them once the electric charge touched them.

"We'll use the light charges when we're killing elephants for their tusks," said Tom, "and the heavy ones when we're in danger from a rush of the beasts."

He little knew how soon he would have to put his plan into effect.

They arrived safely at Majumba, the African coast city, and for two days Tom was kept busy superintending the unloading of the parts of his airship. But it was safely taken ashore, and he and his friends hired a disused warehouse in which to work at reassembling the Black Hawk.

Tom had everything down to a system, and, in less than a week the aircraft was once more ready to be sent aloft. It was given a try- out, much to the astonishment of the natives, and worked perfectly. Then Tom and his friends busied themselves laying in a stock of provisions and stores for the trip into the interior.

They made inquiries about the chances of getting ivory and were told that they were good if they went far enough into the jungle and forests, for the big beasts had penetrated farther and farther inland.

They also tried to get some news regarding the captive missionaries, but were unsuccessful nor could they learn what had become of Tomba, who had brought the dire news to civilization.

"It's too soon to hope for anything yet," said Mr. Anderson. "Wait until we get near the country of the red pygmies."

"And then it may be too late," said Tom in a low voice.

It was two weeks after their arrival in Majumba that Tom announced that all was in readiness. The airship was in perfect working order, it was well stocked with food, arms, articles and trinkets with which to trade among the natives, spare parts for the machinery, special tools and a good supply of the chemicals needed to manufacture the lifting gas.

Of course Tom did not leave behind his electric weapon and Mr. Durban and the others took plenty of ammunition for the ordinary rifles which they carried.

One morning, after cabling to his father that they were about to start, Tom gave a last careful look to his airship, tested the motor and dynamos, took a hasty survey of the storeroom, to see that nothing had been forgotten, and gave the word to get aboard.

They took their places in the cabin. Outside a crowd of natives, and white traders of many nationalities had gathered. Tom pulled the starting lever. The Black Hawk shot across a specially prepared starting ground, and, attaining sufficient momentum, suddenly arose into the air.

There was a cheer from the watching crowd, and several superstitious blacks, who saw the airship for the first time, ran away in terror.

Up into the blue atmosphere Tom took his craft. He looked down on the city over which he was flying. Then he pointed the prow of the Black Hawk toward the heart of the dark continent.

"Off for the interior!" he murmured. "I wonder if we'll ever get out again?"

No one could answer. They had to take their chances with the dangers and terrors of elephant land, and with the red pygmies. Yet Tom Swift was not afraid.

CHAPTER XI

ANCHORED TO EARTH

With the voyage on the steamer, their arrival in Africa, the many strange sights of the city of Majumba, and the refitting of the airship, our friends had hardly had time to catch their breath since Tom Swift's determination to go elephant hunting. Now, as the Black Hawk was speeding into the interior, they felt, for the first time in many weeks, that they "could take it easy," as Ned Newton expressed it.

"Thank goodness," said the bank clerk, "I can sit down and look at something for a while," and he gazed out of the main cabin windows down at the wild country over which they were then flying.

For, so swiftly had the airship moved that it was hardly any time at all before it had left Majumba far behind, and was scudding over the wilderness.

"Bless my camera," exclaimed Mr. Damon, who had brought along one of the picture machines, "bless my camera! I don't call that much to look at," and he pointed to the almost impenetrable forest over which they then were.

"No, it isn't much of a view," said the old elephant hunter, "but wait. You'll soon see all you want to. Africa isn't all like this. There are many strange sights before us yet. But, Tom Swift, tell us how the airship is working in this climate. Do you find any difficulty managing it?"

"Not at all," answered Tom, who was in the cabin then, having set the automatic steering apparatus in the pilot house, and come back to join the others. "It works as well as it did in good old York State. Of course I can't tell what affect the continual hot and moist air will have on the gas bag, but I guess we'll make out all right."

"I certainly hope so," put in Mr. Anderson. "It would be too bad to be wrecked in the middle of Africa, with no way to get out."

"Oh, you needn't worry about that," said Ned with a laugh. "If the airship should smash, Tom would build another out of what was left, and we'd sail away as good as before."

"Hardly that," answered the young inventor.

"But we won't cross a bridge until we hear it coming, as Eradicate would say. Hello, that looks like some sort of native village."

He pointed ahead to a little clearing in the forest, where a number of mud and grass huts were scattered about. As they came nearer they could see the black savages, naked save for a loin cloth, running about in great excitement, and pointing upward.

"Yes, that's one of the numerous small native villages we'll see from now on," said Mr. Durban. "Many a night have I spent in those same grass huts after a day's hunting. Sometimes, I've been comfortable, and again not. I guess we've given those fellows a scare."

It did seem so, for by this time the whole population, including women and children, were running about like mad. Suddenly, from below there sounded a deep booming noise, which came plainly to the ears of the elephant hunters through the opened windows of the airship cabin.

"Hark! What's that?" cried Tom, raising his hand for silence.

"Bless my umbrella! it sounds like thunder," said Mr. Damon.

"No, it's one of their war drums," explained Mr. Durban. "The natives make large ones out of hollow trees, with animal skins stretched over the ends, and they beat them to sound a warning, or before going into battle. It makes a great noise."

"Do you think they want to fight us?" asked Ned, looking anxiously at Tom, and then toward where his rifle stood in a corner of the cabin.

"No, probably that drum was beaten by some of the native priests," explained the hunter. "The natives are very superstitious, and likely they took us for an evil spirit, and wanted to drive us away."

"Then we'll hustle along out of their sight," said Tom, as he went to the pilot house to increase the speed of the airship, for he had been letting it drift along slowly to enable the adventurers to view the country over which they were passing. A few minutes later, under the increased force of the machinery, the Black Hawk left the native village, and the crowd of frightened blacks, far behind.

The travelers passed over a succession of wild stretches of forest or jungle, high above big grassy plains, over low but rugged mountain ranges, and big rivers. Now and then they would cross some lake, on the calm surface of which could be made out natives, in big canoes, hollowed out from trees. In each case the blacks showed every appearance of fright at the sight of the airship throbbing along over their heads.

On passing over the lake, Ned Newton looked down and cried out excitedly:

"Look! Elephants! They're in swimming, and the natives are shooting them! Now's our chance, Tom!"

Mr. Anderson and Mr. Durban, after a quick glance, drew back laughing.

"Those are hippopotami!" exclaimed the old elephant man. "Good hunting, if you don't care what you shoot, but not much sport in it. It will be some time yet before we see any elephants, boys."

Ned was rather chagrined at his mistake, but the African travelers told him that any one, not familiar with the country, would have made it, especially in looking down from a great height.

They sailed along about half a mile above the earth, Tom gradually increasing the speed of the ship, as he found the machinery to be working well. Dinner was served as they were crossing a high grassy plateau, over which could be seen bounding a number of antelopes.

"Some of those would go good for a meal," said Mr. Durban, after a pause during which he watched the graceful creatures.

"Then we'll go down and get some for supper," decided Tom, for in that hot climate it was impossible to carry fresh meat on the airship.

Accordingly, the Black Hawk was sent down, and came to rest in a natural clearing on the edge of the jungle. After waiting until the fierce heat of noonday was over, the travelers got out their rifles and, under the leadership of Mr. Durban and Mr. Anderson, who was also an experienced hunter, they set off.

Game was plentiful, but as they could only eat a comparatively small quantity, and as it would not keep, they only shot what they needed. Tom had his electric rifle, but hesitated to use it, as Mr. Durban and Mr. Anderson had each already bowled over a fine buck.

However, a chance came most unexpectedly, for, as they were passing along the banks of a little stream, which was almost hidden from view by thick weeds and rank grass, there was a sudden commotion in the bushes, and a fierce wild buffalo sprang out at the party.

There are few animals in Africa more dreaded by hunters than the wild buffalo, for the beast, with its spreading sharp horns is a formidable foe, and will seldom give up the attack until utterly unable to move. They are fierce and relentless.

"Look out!" yelled Mr. Durban. "To cover, everybody! If that beast gets after you it's no fun! You and I will fire at him, Mr. Anderson!"

Mr. Durban raised his rifle, and pulled the trigger, but, for some reason, the weapon failed to go off. Mr. Anderson quickly raised his, but his foot slipped in a wet place and he fell. At that moment the buffalo, with a snort of rage, charged straight for the fallen man.

"Tom! your electric rifle!" yelled Ned Newton, but he need not have done so, for the young inventor was on the alert.

Taking instant aim, and adjusting his weapon for the heaviest charge, Tom fired at the advancing beast. The result was the same as in the case of the whale, the buffalo seemed to melt away. And it was stopped only just in time, too, for it was close to the prostrate Mr. Anderson, who had sprained his ankle slightly, and could not readily rise.

It was all over in a few seconds, but it was a tense time while it lasted.

"You saved my life again, Tom Swift," said Mr. Anderson, as he limped toward our hero. "Once on Earthquake Island, and again now. I shan't forget it," and he shook hands with the young inventor.

The others congratulated Tom on his quick shot, and Mr. Damon, as usual blessed everything in sight, and the electric rifle especially.

They went back to the airship, taking the fresh meat with them, but on account of the injury to Mr. Anderson's ankle could not make quick progress, so that it was almost dusk when they reached the craft.

"Well, we'll have supper, and then start off," proposed Tom, "I don't think it would be wise to remain on the ground so near the jungle."

"No' it's safer in the air," agreed Mr. Durban. The meal was much enjoyed, especially the fresh meat, and, after it was over, Tom took his place in the pilot house to start the machinery, and send the airship aloft.

The motor hummed and throbbed, and the gas hissed into the bag, for the ground was not level enough to permit of a running start by means of the planes. Lights gleamed from the Black Hawk and the big search-lantern in front cast a dazzling finger of light into the black forest.

"Well, what are you waiting for?" called Ned, who heard the machinery in motion, but who could not feel the craft rising. "Why don't you go up, Tom?"

"I'm trying to," answered the young inventor. "Something seems to be the matter." He pulled the speed lever over a few more notches, and increased the power of the gas machine. Still the Black Hawk did not rise.

"Bless my handkerchief box!" cried Mr. Damon, "what's the matter?"

"I don't know," answered Tom. "We seem to be held fast."

He further increased the speed of the propellers, and the gas machine was set to make vapor at its fullest capacity, and force it into the bag. Still the craft was held to the earth.

"Maybe the gas has no effect in this climate," called Ned.

"It can't be that," replied Tom. "The gas will operate anywhere. It worked all right today."

Suddenly she airship moved up a little way, and then seemed to be pulled down again, hitting the ground with a bump.

"Something is holding us!" cried Tom. "We're anchored to earth! I must see what it is!" and, catching up his electric rifle, he dashed out of the cabin.

CHAPTER XII

AMONG THE NATIVES

For a moment after Tom's departure the others stared blankly at one another. They could hear the throbbing and hum of the machinery, and feel the thrill of the anchored airship. But they could not understand what the trouble was.

"We must help Tom!" cried Ned Newton at length as he caught up his rifle. "Maybe we are in the midst of a herd of elephants, and they have hold of the ship in their trunks."

"It couldn't be!" declared Mr. Durban, yet they soon discovered that Ned's guess was nearer the truth then any of them had suspected at the time.

"We must help him, true enough!" declared Mr. Anderson, and he and the others followed Ned out on deck.

"Where are you Tom?" called his chum.

"Here." was the answer. "I'm on the forward deck."

"Do you see anything?"

"No, it's too dark. Turn the search-light this way."

"I will," shouted Mr. Damon, and a moment later the gleam of the powerful lantern brought Tom clearly into view, as he stood on the small forward observation platform in the bow of the Black Hawk.

An instant later the young inventor let out a startled cry.

"What is it?" demanded Mr. Durban.

"An immense snake!" shouted Tom. "It's wound around a tree, and partly twined around the ship! That's why we couldn't go up! I'm going to shoot it."

They looked to where he pointed, and there, in the glare of the light, could be seen an immense python, fully twenty-five feet long, the forward part of its fat ugly body circled around the slender prow of the airship, while the folds of the tail were about a big tree.

Tom Swift raised his electric rifle, took quick aim, and, having set it to deliver a moderate charge, pressed the button. The result was surprising, for the snake being instantly killed the folds uncoiled and the ship shot upward, only, instead of rising on an even keel, the bow pointed toward the sky, while the stern was still fast to the earth. Tilted at an angle of forty-five degrees the Black Hawk was in a most peculiar position, and those standing on the deck began to slide along it.

"There's another snake at the stern!" cried Mr. Damon as he grasped a brace to prevent falling off. "Bless my slippers! it's the mate of the one you killed! Shoot the other one, Tom!"

The young inventor needed no urging. Making his way as best he could to the stern of the airship, he killed the second python, which was even larger than the first, and in an instant the Black Hawk shot upward, this time level, and as it should be. Things on board were soon righted, and the travelers could stand upright. High above the black jungle rose the craft, moving forward under the full power of the propellers, until Tom rushed into the engine room, and reduced speed.

"Well, talk about things happening!" exclaimed Ned, when they had somewhat recovered from the excitement. "I should say they were beginning with a vengeance!"

"That's the way in Africa," declared Mr. Durban. "It's a curious country. Those pythons generally go in pairs, but it's the first time I ever knew them to tackle an airship. They probably stay around here where there is plenty of small game for them, and very likely they merely anchored to our craft while waiting for a supper to come along."

"It was a very odd thing," said Tom. "I couldn't imagine what held us. After this I'll see that all is clear before I try to go up. Next time we may be held by a troop of baboons and it strains the machinery to have it pull against dead weight in that way."

However, it was found no harm had resulted from this experience, and, after reducing the gas pressure, which was taking them too high, Tom set the automatic rudders.

"We'll keep on at slow speed through the night," he explained, "and in the morning we'll be pretty well into the interior. Then we can lay our course for wherever we want to go. Where had we better head for?"

"I don't want to interfere with your plans," said Mr. Anderson, "but I would like to rescue those missionaries. But the trouble is, I don't know just where to look for them. We couldn't get much of a line in Majumba on where the country of the red pygmies is located. What do you think about it, Mr. Durban?"

"As far as elephant hunting goes we can probably do as well in the pygmy land as anywhere else," answered the veteran, "and perhaps it will be well to head for that place. If we run across any elephant herds in the meanwhile, we can stop, get the ivory, and proceed."

They discussed this plan at some length, and agreed that it was the best thing to do. Mr. Durban had a map of the country around the center of Africa, and he marked on it, as nearly as he could, the location of the pygmies' country, while Mr. Anderson also had a chart, showing the location of the mission which had been wiped out of existence. It was in the midst of a wild and desolate region.

"We'll do the best we can," declared Tom, "and I think we'll succeed. We ought to be there in about a week, if we have no bad luck."

All that night the Black Hawk flew on over Africa, covering mile after mile, passing over jungle, forest, plains, rivers and lakes, and, doubtless, over many native villages, though they could not be seen.

Morning found the travelers above a great, grassy plain, dotted here and there with negro settlements which were separated by rivers, lakes or thin patches of forest.

“Well, we’ll speed up a bit,” decided Tom after breakfast, which was eaten to the weird accompaniment of hundreds of native warning- drums, beaten by the superstitious blacks.

Tom went to the engine room, and turned on more speed. He was about to go back to the pilot house, to set the automatic steering apparatus to coincide with the course mapped out, when there was a crash of metal, an ominous snapping and buzzing sound, followed by a sudden silence.

“What’s that?” cried Ned, who was in the motor compartment with his chum.

“Something’s gone wrong!” exclaimed the young inventor, as he sprang back toward the engine. The propellers had ceased revolving, and as there was no gas in the bag at that time, it having been decided to save the vapor for future needs, the Black Hawk began falling toward the earth.

“We’re going down!” yelled Ned.

“Yes, the main motor has broken!” exclaimed Tom. “We’ll have to descend to repair it.”

“Say!” yelled Mr. Damon, rushing in, “we’re right over a big African village! Are we going to fall among the natives?”

“It looks that way,” admitted Tom grimly, as he hastened to the pilot house to shift the wings so that the craft could glide easily to the ground.

“Bless my shoe blacking!” cried the eccentric man as he heard the beating of drums, and the shouts of the savages.

A little later the airship had settled into the midst of a crowd of Africans, who swarmed all about the craft.

CHAPTER XIII

ON AN ELEPHANT TRAIL

"Get ready with your guns, everybody!" cried the old elephant hunter, as he prepared to leave the cabin of the Black Hawk. "Tom Swift, don't forget your electric rifle. There'll be trouble soon!"

"Bless my cartridge belt!" gasped Mr. Damon. "Why? What will happen?"

"The natives," answered Mr. Durban. "They'll attack us sure as fate! See, already they're getting out their bows and arrows, and blowguns! They'll pierce the gas bag in a hundred places!"

"If they do, it will be a bad thing for us," muttered Tom. "We can't have that happen."

He followed the old elephant hunter outside, and Mr. Anderson, Ned Newton and Mr. Damon trailed after, each one with a gun, while Tom had his electric weapon. The airship rested on its wheels on some level ground, just in front of a large hut, surrounded by a number of smaller ones. All about were the natives, tall, gaunt black men, hideous in their savagery, wearing only the loin cloth, and with their kinky hair stuck full of sticks, bones and other odd objects they presented a curious sight.

Some of them were dancing about, brandishing their weapons—clubs spears, bows, and arrows, or the long, slender blowguns, consisting merely of a hollow reed. Women and children there were, too, also dancing and leaping about, howling at the tops of their voices. Above the unearthly din could be heard the noise of the drums and tom-toms, while, as the adventurers drew up in front of their airship, there came a sort of chant, and a line of natives, dressed fantastically in the skins of beasts, came filing out of the large hut.

"The witch-doctors!" exclaimed Tom, who had read of them in African travel books.

"Are they going to attack us?" cried Ned.

"Bless my hymn book! I hope not!" came from Mr. Damon. "We wouldn't have any chance at all in this horde of black men. I wish Eradicate Sampson and his mule Boomerang were here. Maybe he could talk their language, and tell them that we meant no harm."

"If there's any talking to be done, I guess our guns will have to do it," said Tom grimly.

"I can speak a little of their language," remarked Mr. Durban, "but what in the world are the beggars up to, anyhow? I supposed they'd send a volley of arrows at us, first shot, but they don't seem to be going to do that."

"No, they're dancing around us," said Tom.

"That's it!" exclaimed Mr. Anderson. "I have it! Why didn't I think of it before? The natives are welcoming us!"

"Welcoming us?" repeated Ned.

"Yes," went on the missionary seeker. "They are doing a dance in our honor, and they have even called out the witch-doctors to do us homage."

"That's right," agreed Mr. Durban, who was listening to the chanting of the natives dressed in animal skins. "They take us for spirits from another land, and are making us welcome here. Listen, I'll see if I can make out what else they are saying."

The character of the shouts and chants changed abruptly, and the dancing increased in fervor, even the children throwing themselves wildly about. The witch-doctors ran around like so many maniacs, and it looked as much like an American Indian war dance as anything else.

"I've got it!" shouted Mr. Durban, for he had to call loudly to be heard above the din. "They are asking us to make it rain. It seems there has been a dry spell here, and their own rain-makers and witch-doctors haven't been able to get a drop out of the sky. Now, they take it that we have come to help them. They think we are going to bring rain."

"And if we don't, what will happen?" asked Tom.

"Maybe they won't be quite so glad to see us," was the answer.

"Well, if they don't mean war, we might as well put up our weapons," suggested Mr. Anderson. "If they're going to be friendly, so much the better, and if it should happen to rain while we're here, they'd think we brought it, and we could have almost anything we wanted. Perhaps they have a store of ivory hidden away, Mr. Durban. Some of these tribes do."

"It's possible, but the chances for rain are very small. How long will we have to stay here, Tom Swift?" asked the elephant hunter anxiously.

"Well, perhaps I can get the motor mended in two or three days," answered the young inventor.

"Then we'll have to stay here in the meanwhile," decided Mr. Durban. "Well, we'll make the best of it. Ha, here comes the native king to do us honor," and, as he spoke there came toward the airship a veritable giant of a black man, wearing a leopard skin as a royal garment, while on his head was a much battered derby hat, probably purchased at a fabulous price from some trader. The king, if such he could be called, was accompanied by a number of attendants and witch-doctors. In front walked a small man, who, as it developed, was an interpreter. The little cavalcade advanced close to the airship, and came to a halt. The king made a low bow, either to the craft or to the elephant hunters drawn up in front of it. His attendants followed his example, and then the interpreter began to speak.

Mr. Durban listened intently, made a brief answer to the little man, and then the elephant hunter's face lighted up.

"It's all right," he said to Tom and the others. "The king takes us for wonderful spirits from another land. He welcomes us, says we can have whatever we want, and he begs us to make it rain. I have said we will do our best, and I have asked that some food be sent us. That's always the first thing to do. We'll be allowed to stay here in peace until Tom can mend the ship, and then we'll hit the air trail again."

The talk between Mr. Durban and the interpreter continued for some little time longer. Then the king went back to his hut, refusing, as Mr. Durban said, an invitation to come aboard and see how a modern airship was constructed. The natives, too, seemed anxious to give the craft a wide berth.

The excitement had quieted down now, and, in a short time a crowd of native women came toward the airship, bearing, in baskets on their heads, food of various kinds. There were bananas, some wild fruits, yams, big gourds of goats' milk, some boiled and stewed flesh of young goats, nicely cooked, and other things, the nature of which could only be guessed at.

"Shall we eat this stuff, or stick to Mr. Damon's cooking?" asked Tom.

"Oh, you'll find this very good," explained Mr. Durban. "I've eaten native cookery before. Some of it is excellent and as this appears to be very good, Mr. Damon can have a vacation while we are here."

The old elephant hunter proved the correctness of his statement by beginning to eat, and soon all the travelers were partaking of the food left by the native women. They placed it down on the ground at a discreet distance from the airship, and hurriedly withdrew. But if the women and men were afraid, the children were not, and they were soon swarming about the ship, timidly touching the sides with their little black fingers, but not venturing on board.

Tom, with Ned and Mr. Damon to help him, began work on the motor right after dinner. He found the break to be worse than he had supposed, and knew that it would take at least four days to repair it.

Meanwhile the airship continued to be a source of wonder to the natives. They were always about it, save at night, but their admiration was a respectful one. The king was anxious for the rain-making incantations to begin, but Mr. Durban put him off.

"I don't want to deceive these simple natives," he said, "and for our own safety we can't pretend to make rain, and fail. As soon as we have a chance we'll slip away from here."

But an unexpected happening made a change in their plans. It was on the afternoon of their third day in the native village, and Tom and his assistants were working hard at the motor. Suddenly there seemed to be great excitement in the vicinity of the king's hut. A native had rushed into the village from the jungle, evidently with some news, for presently the whole place was in a turmoil.

Once more the king and his attendants filed out toward the airship. Once more the interpreter talked to Mr. Durban, who listened eagerly.

"By Jove! here's our chance!" he cried to Tom, when the little man had finished.

"What is it?" asked the young inventor.

"A runner has just come in with news that a large herd of wild elephants is headed this way. The king is afraid the big beasts will trample down all their crops, as often occurs, and he begs us to go out and drive the animals away. It's just what we want. Come on, Tom, and all of you. The airship will be safe here, for the natives think that to meddle with it would mean death or enchantment for then. We'll get on our first elephant trail!"

The old hunter went into the cabin for his big game gun, while Tom hastened to get out his electric rifle. Now he would have a chance to try it on the powerful beasts which he had come to Africa to hunt.

Amid the excited and joyous shouts of the natives, the hunters filed out of the village, led by the dusky messenger who had brought the news of the elephants. And, as Tom and the others advanced, they could hear a distant trumpeting, and a crashing in the jungle that told of the near presence of the great animals.

CHAPTER XIV

A STAMPEDE

"Look to your guns, everybody!" cautioned Mr. Durban. "It's no joke to be caught in an elephant herd with an unloaded rifle. Have you plenty of ammunition, Mr. Damon?"

"Ammunition? Bless my powder bag, I think I have enough for all the elephants I'll kill. If I get one of the big beasts I'll be satisfied. Bless my piano keys! I think I see them, Tom!"

He pointed off through the thick jungle. Surely something was moving there amid the trees; great slate-colored bodies, massive forms and waving trunks! The trumpeting increased, and the crashing of the underbrush sounded louder and nearer.

"There they are!" cried Tom Swift joyously.

"Now for my first big game!" yelled Ned Newton.

"Take it easy," advised Mr. Anderson. "Remember to aim for the spot I mentioned to you as being the best, just at the base of the skull. If you can't make a head shot, or through the eye, try for the heart. But with the big bullets we have, almost any kind of a shot, near a vital spot, will answer."

"And Tom can fire at their TOES and put them out of business," declared Ned, who was eagerly advancing. "How about it, Tom?"

"Well, I guess the electric rifle will come up to expectations. Say, Mr. Durban, they seem to be heading this way!" excitedly cried Tom, as the herd of big beasts suddenly turned and changed their course.

"Yes, they are," admitted the old elephant hunter calmly. "But that won't matter. Take it easy. Kill all you can."

"But we don't want to put too many out of business," said Tom, who was not needlessly cruel, even in hunting.

"I know that," answered Mr. Durban. "But this is a case of necessity. I've got to get ivory, and we have to kill quite a few elephants to accomplish this. Besides the brutes will head for the village and the natives' grain fields, and trample them down, if they're not headed back. So all together now, we'll give them a volley. This is a good place! There they are. All line up now. Get ready!"

He halted, and the others followed his example. The natives had come to a stop some time before, and were huddled together in the jungle back of our friends, waiting to see the result of the white men's shots.

Tom, Ned, Mr. Damon, and the two older hunters were on an irregular line in the forest. Before them was the mass of elephants advancing slowly, and feeding on the tender leaves of trees as they came on. They would reach up with their long trunks, strip off the foliage, and stuff it into their mouths. Sometimes, they even pulled up small trees by the roots for the purpose of stripping them more easily.

"Jove! There are some big tuskers in that bunch!" cried Mr. Durban. "Aim for the bulls, every one, don't kill the mothers or little ones." Tom now saw that there were a number of baby Elephants in the herd, and he appreciated the hunter's desire to spare them and their mothers.

"Here we go!" exclaimed Mr. Durban, as he saw that Tom and the others were ready. "Aim! Fire!"

There were thundering reports that awoke the echoes of the jungle, and the sounds of the rifles were followed by shrill trumpets of rage. When the smoke blew away three elephants were seen prostrate, or, rather two, and part of another one. The last was almost blown to pieces by Tom Swift's electric rifle; for the young inventor had used a little too heavy charge, and the big beast had been almost annihilated.

Mr. Durban had dropped his bull with a well-directed shot, and Mr. Anderson had a smaller one to his credit.

"I guess I missed mine," said Ned ruefully.

"Bless my dress-suit case!" exclaimed Mr. Damon. "So did I!"

"One of you hit that fellow!" cried Mr. Durban. "He's wounded."

He pointed to a fair-sized bull who was running wildly about, uttering shrill cries of anger. The other beasts had gathered in a compact mass, with the larger bulls, or tuskers, on the outside, to protect the females and young.

"I'll try a shot at him," said Tom, and raising his electric, gun, he took quick aim. The elephant dropped in his tracks, for this time the young inventor had correctly adjusted the power of the wireless bullet.

"Good!" cried Mr. Durban. "Give them some more! This is some of the best ivory I've seen yet!"

As he spoke he fired, and bowled over another magnificent specimen. Ned Newton, determined to make a record of at least one, fired again, and to his delight, saw a big fellow drop.

"I got him!" he yelled.

Mr. Anderson also got another, and then Mr. Damon, blessing something which his friends could not make out, fired at one of the largest bulls in the herd.

"You only nipped him!" exclaimed Mr. Durban when the smoke had drifted away. "I guess I'll put him out of his misery!"

He raised his weapon and pulled the trigger but no report followed. He uttered an exclamation of dismay.

“The breech-action has jammed!” he exclaimed. “Drop him, Tom. He’s scented us, and is headed this way. The whole herd will follow in a minute.”

Already the big brute wounded by Mr. Damon had trumpeted out a cry of rage and defiance. It was echoed by his mates. Then, with upraised trunk, he darted forward, followed by a score of big tuskers.

But Tom had heard and understood. The leading beast had not taken three steps before he dropped under the deadly and certain fire of the young inventor.

“Bless my wishbone!” cried Mr. Damon when he saw how effective the electric weapon was.

There was a shout of joy from the natives in the rear. They saw the slain creatures and knew there would be much fresh meat and feasting for them for days to come.

Suddenly Mr. Durban cried out: “Fire again, Tom! Fire everybody! The whole herd is coming this way. If we don’t stop them they’ll overrun the fields and village, and may smash the airship! Fire again!”

Almost as he spoke, the rush, which had been stopped momentarily, when Tom dropped the wounded elephant, began again. With shrill menacing cries the score of bulls in the lead came on, followed this time by the females and the young.

“It’s a stampede!” yelled Mr. Anderson, firing into the midst of the herd. Mr. Durban was working frantically at his clogged rifle. Ned and Mr. Damon both fired, and Tom Swift, adjusting his weapon to give the heaviest charges, shot a fusillade of wireless bullets into the center of the advancing elephants, who were now wild with fear and anger.

“It’s a stampede all right!” said Tom, when he saw that the big creatures were not going to stop, in spite of the deadly fire poured into them.

CHAPTER XV

LIONS IN THE NIGHT

Shouting, screaming, imploring their deities in general, and the white men in particular for protection, the band of frightened natives broke and ran through the jungle, caring little where they went so long as they escaped the awful terror of the pursuing herd of maddened elephants. Behind them came Tom Swift and the others, for it were folly to stop in the path of the infuriated brutes.

"Our only chance is to get on their flank and try to turn them!" yelled Mr. Durban. "We may beat them in getting to the clearing, for the trail is narrow. Run, everybody!"

No one needed his excited advice to cause them to hurry. They scudded along, Mr. Damon's cap falling off in his haste. But he did not stop to pick it up.

The hunters had one advantage. They were on a narrow but well-cleared trail through the jungle, which led from the village where they were encamped, to another, several miles away. This trail was too small for the elephants, and, indeed, had to be taken in single file by the travelers.

But it prevented the elephants making the same speed as did our friends, for the jungle, at this point, consisted of heavy trees, which halted the progress of even the strongest of the powerful beasts. True, they could force aside the frail underbrush and the small trees, but the others impeded their progress.

"We'll get there ahead of them!" cried Tom. "Have you got your rifle in working order yet, Mr. Durban?"

"No, something has broken, I fear. We'll have to depend on your electric gun, Tom. Have you many charges left?"

"A dozen or so. But Ned and the others have plenty of ammunition."

"Don't count—on—me!" panted Mr. Damon, who was well-nigh breathless from the run. "I—can't—aim—straight—any—more!"

"I'll give 'em a few more bullets!" declared Mr. Anderson.

The fleeing natives were now almost lost to sight, for they could travel through the jungle, ignoring the trail, at high speed. They were almost like snakes or animals in this respect. Their one thought was to get to their village, and, if possible, protect their huts and fields of grain from annihilation by the elephants.

Behind our friends, trumpeting, bellowing and crashing came the pachyderms. They seemed to be gaining, and Tom, looking back, saw one big brute emerge upon the trail, and follow that.

"I've got to stop him, or some of the others will do the same," thought the young inventor. He halted and fired quickly. The elephant seemed to melt away, and Tom with regret, saw a pair of fine tusks broken to bits. "I used too heavy a charge," he murmured, as he took up the retreat again.

In a few minutes the party of hunters, who were now playing more in the role of the hunted, came out into the open. They could hear the natives beating on their big hollow tree drums, and on tom-toms, while the witch-doctors and medicine men were chanting weird songs to drive the elephants away.

But the beasts came on. One by one they emerged from the jungle, until the herd was gathered together again in a compact mass. Then, under the leadership of some big bulls, they advanced. It seemed as if they knew what they were doing, and were determined to revenge themselves by trampling the natives' huts under their ponderous feet.

But Tom and the others were not idle. Taking a position off to one side, the young inventor began pouring a fusillade of the electric bullets into the mass of slate-colored bodies. Mr. Anderson was also firing, and Ned, who had gotten over some of his excitement, was also doing execution. Mr. Durban, after vainly trying to get his rifle to work, cast it aside. "Here! Let me take your gun!" he cried to Mr. Damon, who, panting from the run, was sitting beneath a tree.

"Bless my cartridge belt! Take it and welcome!" assented the eccentric man. It still had several shots in the magazine, and these the old hunter used with good effect.

At first it seemed as if the elephants could not be turned back. They kept on rushing toward the village, which was not far away, and Tom and the others followed at one side, as best they could, firing rapidly. The electric rifle did fearful execution.

Emboldened by the fear that all their possessions would be destroyed a body of the natives rushed out, right in front of the elephants, and beat tom-toms and drums, almost under their feet, at the same time singing wild songs.

"I'm afraid we can't stop them!" muttered Mr. Anderson. "We'd better hurry to the airship, and protect that, Tom."

But, almost as he spoke, the tide of battle turned. The elephants suddenly swung about, and began a retreat. They could not stand the hot fire of the four guns, including Tom's fearful weapon. With wild trumpetings they fled back into the jungle, leaving a number of their dead behind.

"A close call," murmured Tom, as he drew a breath of relief. Indeed this was true, for the tide had turned when the foremost elephants were not a hundred feet away from the first rows of native huts.

"I should say it was," agreed Ned Newton, wiping his face with his handkerchief. He, as well as the others, was an odd-looking sight. They were blackened by powder smoke, scratched by briars, and red from exertion.

"But we got more ivory in this hour than I could have secured in a week of ordinary hunting," declared Mr. Durban. "If this keeps up we won't have to get much more, except that I don't think any of the tusks to-day are large enough for the special purpose of my customer."

"The sooner we get enough ivory the quicker we can go to the rescue of the missionaries," said Mr. Anderson.

"That's so," remarked Tom. "We must not forget the red pygmies."

The natives were now dancing about, wild in delight at the prospect of unlimited eating, and also thankful for what the white men had done for them. Alone, the blacks would never have been able to stop the stampede. They were soon busy cutting up the elephants ready for a big feast, and runners were sent to tell neighboring tribes, in adjoining villages, of the delights awaiting them.

Mr. Durban gave instructions about saving the ivory tusks, and the valuable teeth, each pair worth about $1,000, were soon cut out and put away for our friends. Some had been lost by the excessive power of Tom's gun, but this could not be helped. It was necessary to stop the rush at any price.

There was soon a busy scene at the native village, and with the arrival of other tribesmen it seemed as if Bedlam had broken loose. The blacks chattered like so many children as they prepared for the feast.

"Do white men ever eat elephant meat?" asked Mr. Damon, as the adventurers were gathered about the airship.

"Indeed they do," declared Mr. Durban. "Baked elephant foot is a delicacy that few appreciate. I'll have the natives cook some for us."

He gave the necessary orders, and the travelers had to admit that it was worth coming far to get.

For the next few days and nights there was great feasting in that African village, and the praises of the white men, and power of Tom Swift's electric rifle, were sung loud and long.

Our friends had resumed work on repairing the airship, and the young inventor declared, one night, that they could proceed the next day.

They were seated around a small campfire, watching the dancing and antics of some natives who were at their usual work of eating meat. All about our friends were numerous blazes for the cooking of the feasts, and some were on the very edge of the jungle.

Suddenly, above the uncouth sounds of the merry-making, there was heard a deep vibration and roar, not unlike the distant rumble of thunder or the hum of a great steamer's whistle heard afar in the fog.

"What's that?" cried Ned.

"Lions," said Mr. Durban briefly. "They have been attracted by the smell of cooking."

At that moment, and instantly following a very loud roar, there was an agonized scream of pain and terror. It sounded directly in back of the airship.

"A lion!" cried Mr. Anderson. "One of the brutes has grabbed a native!"

Tom Swift caught up his rifle, and darted off toward the dark jungle.

CHAPTER XVI

SEEKING THE MISSIONARIES

"Here! Come back!" yelled Mr. Damon and Mr. Anderson, in the same breath, while the old elephant hunter cried out: "Don't you know you're risking your life, Tom to go off in the dark, to trail a lion?"

"I can't stand it to let the native be carried off!" Tom shouted back.

"But you can't see in the dark," objected Mr. Anderson. He had probably forgotten the peculiar property of the electric rifle. Tom kept on, and the others slowly followed.

The natives had at once ceased their merrymaking at the roaring of the lions, and now all were gathered close about the campfires, on which more wood had been piled, to drive away the fearsome brutes.

"There must be a lot of them," observed Mr. Durban, as menacing growls and roars came from the jungle, along the edge of which Tom and the others were walking just then. "There are so many of the brutes that they are bold, and they must be hungry, too. They came close to our fire, because it wasn't so bright as the other blazes, and that native must have wandered off into the forest. Well, I guess it's all up with him."

"He's screaming yet," observed Ned.

Indeed, above the rumbling roars of the lions, and the crackling of the campfires, could be heard the moaning cries of the unfortunate black.

"He's right close here!" suddenly called Tom. "He's skirting the jungle. I think I can get him!"

"Don't take any risks!" called Mr. Durban, who had caught up his own rifle, that was now in working order again.

Tom Swift was not in sight. He had now penetrated into the jungle— into the black forest where stalked the savage lions, intent on getting other prey. Mr. Durban and Mr. Anderson vainly tried to pierce the darkness to see something at which to shoot. Ned Newton had eagerly started to follow his chum, but could not discern where Tom was. A nameless fear clutched at the lad's heart. Mr. Damon was softly blessing everything of which he could think.

Once more came that pitiful cry from the native, who was, as they afterward learned, being dragged along by the lion, who had grabbed him by the shoulder.

Suddenly in the dense jungle there shone a purple-bluish light. It illuminated the scene like some great sky-rocket for an instant, and in that brief time Ned and the others caught sight of a great, tawny form, bounding along. It was a lion, with head held high, dragging along a helpless black man.

A second later, and before the intense glare had died away, the watchers saw the lion gently sink down, as though weary. He stopped short in his tracks, his head rolled back, the jaws relaxed and the native, who was unconscious now, toppled to one side.

"Tom's killed him with the electric rifle!" cried Mr. Durban.

"Bless my incandescent lamp! so he has," agreed Mr. Damon. "Bless my dynamo! but that's a wonderful gun, it's as powerful as a thunderbolt, or as gentle as a summer shower."

Mr. Durban seeing that the lion was dead, in that brief glance he had had of the brute, called to some of the natives to come and get their tribesman. They came, timidly enough at first, carrying many torches, but when they understood that the lion was dead, they advanced more boldly. They carried the wounded black to a hut, where they applied their simple but effective remedies for the cruel bite in his shoulder.

After Tom had shot several other of the illuminated charges into the jungle, to see if he could discover any more lions, but failed to do so, he and his friends returned to the anchored airship, amid the murmured thanks of the Africans.

Bright fires were kept blazing all the rest of the night, but, though lions could be heard roaring in the jungle, and though they approached alarmingly close to the place where our friends were encamped, none of the savage brutes ventured within the clearing.

With the valuable store of ivory aboard the Black Hawk, which was now completely repaired, an early start was made the next morning. The Africans besought Tom and his companions to remain, for it was not often they could have the services of white men in slaying elephants and lions.

"But, we've got to get on the trail," decided Tom, when the natives had brought great stores of food, and such simple presents as they possessed, to induce the travelers to remain.

"Every hour may add to the danger of the missionaries in the hands of the red pygmies."

"Yes," said Mr. Anderson gravely, "it is our duty to save them."

And so the airship mounted into the air, our friends waving farewells to the simple-hearted blacks, who did a sort of farewell war-dance in their honor, shouting their praises aloud, and beating the drums and tom-toms, so that the echoes followed for some time after the Black Hawk had begun to mount upward toward the sky.

The craft was in excellent shape, due to the overhauling Tom had given it while making the repairs. With the propellers beating the air, and the rudder set to hold them about two thousand feet high, the travelers moved rapidly over clearings, forests and jungles.

It was agreed that now, when they had made such a good start in collecting ivory, that they would spend the next few days in trying to get on the trail of the red pygmies. It might seem a simple matter, after knowing the approximate location of the land of these fierce little natives, to have proceeded directly to it. But Africa is an immense continent, and even in an airship comparatively little of the interior can be seen at a time.

Besides, the red pygmies had a habit of moving from place to place, and they were so small, and so wild, capable of living in very tiny huts or caves, and so primitive, not building regular villages as the other Africans do, that as Ned said, they were as hard to locate as the proverbial flea.

Our friends had a general idea of where to look for them, but on nearing that land, and making inquiries of several friendly tribes, they learned that the red pygmies had suddenly disappeared from their usual haunts.

"I guess they heard that we were after them," said Tom, with a grim smile one day, as he sent the airship down toward the earth, for they were over a great plain, and several native villages could be seen dotted on its surface.

"More likely they are in hiding because they have as captives two white persons," said Mr. Anderson. "They are fierce and fearless, but, nevertheless, they have, in times past, felt the vengeance of the white man, and perhaps they dread that now."

They made a descent, and spent several days making inquiries from the friendly blacks about the race of little men. But scarcely anything was learned. Some of the negro tribes admitted having heard of the red pygmies, and others, with superstitious incantations and imprecations, said they had never heard of them.

One tribe of very large negroes had heard a rumor to the effect that the band of the pygmies was several days' journey from their village, across the mountains, and when Tom sent his airship there, the searchers only found an impenetrable jungle, filled with lions and other wild beasts, but not a sign of the pygmies, and with no elephants to reward their search.

"But we're not going to give up," declared Tom, and the others agreed with him. Forward went the Black Hawk in the search for the imprisoned ones, but, as the days passed, and no news was had, it seemed to grow more and more hopeless.

"I'm afraid if we do find them now," remarked Mr. Anderson at length, "that we'll only recover the bodies of the missionaries."

"Then we'll avenge them," said Tom quietly.

They had stopped at another native village to make inquiries, but without result, and were about to start off again that night when a runner came in to announce that a herd of big elephants was feeding not many miles away.

"Well, we'll stay over a day or so, and get some more ivory," decided Mr. Durban and that night they got ready for what was to prove a big hunt.

CHAPTER XVII

SHOTS FROM ABOVE

"There they are!"

"My, what a lot of big ones!"

"Jove! Mr. Anderson, see those tusks!"

"Yes, you ought to get what you want this time, Mr. Durban."

"Bless my hatband! There must be two hundred of them!" exclaimed Mr. Damon.

"I'm glad I recharged my rifle last night!" exclaimed Tom Swift. "It's fully loaded now."

Then followed exulting cries and shouts of the natives, who were following our friends, the elephant hunters, who had given voice to the remarks we have just quoted.

It was early in the morning, and the hunt was about to start, for the news brought in by the runner the night before had been closely followed by the brutes themselves, and at dawn our friends were astir, for scouts brought in word that the elephants, including many big ones, were passing along only a few miles from the African village.

Cautiously approaching, with the wind blowing from the elephants to them, the white hunters made their way along. Mr. Durban was in the lead, and when he saw a favorable opportunity he motioned for the others to advance. Then, when he noticed the big bull sentinels of the herd look about as if to detect the presence of enemies, he gave another signal and the hunters sank out of sight in the tall grass.

As for the natives, they were like snakes, unseen but ever present, wriggling along on their hands and knees. They were awaiting the slaughter, when there would be fresh meat in abundance.

At length the old elephant hunter decided that they were near enough to chance some shots. As a matter of fact, Tom Swift, with his electric rifle, had been within range some time before, but as he did not want to spoil the sport for the others, by firing and killing, and so alarming the herd, he had held back. Now they could all shoot together.

"Let her go!" suddenly cried Mr. Durban, and they took aim.

There was a fusillade of reports and several of the big brutes toppled over.

"Bless my toothbrush!" cried Mr. Damon, "that's the time I got one!"

"Yes, and a fine specimen, too!" added Mr. Durban, who had only succeeded in downing a small bull, with an indifferent pair of tusks. "A fine specimen, Mr. Damon, I congratulate you!"

As for Tom Swift, he had killed two of the largest elephants in the herd.

But now the hunters had their work cut out for them, since the beasts had taken fright and were charging away at what seemed an awkward gait, but which, nevertheless, took them rapidly over the ground.

"Come on!" cried Mr. Durban. "We must get some more. Some of the finest tusks I have ever seen are running away from us!"

He began to race after the retreating herd, but it is doubtful if he would have caught up to them had not a band of natives, who had crept up and surrounded the beasts, turned them by shouts and the beating of tom-toms. Seeing an enemy in front of them, the elephants turned, and our friends were able to get in several more shots. Tom Swift picked out only those with immense tusks, and soon had several to his credit. Ned Newton also bagged some prizes.

But finally the elephants, driven to madness by the firing and the yells of the natives, broke through the line of black men, and charged off into the jungle, where it was not only useless but dangerous to follow them.

"Well, we have enough," said Mr. Durban, and when the tusks had been collected it was found that indeed a magnificent and valuable supply had been gathered.

"But I have yet to get my prize ones," said the old hunter with a sigh. "Maybe we'll find the elephant with them when we locate the red pygmies."

"If we do, we'll have our work cut out for us," declared Tom.

As on the other occasion after the hunt, there was a great feast for the natives, who invited tribes from miles around, and for two days, while the tusks were being cut out and cleaned, there were barbeques on every side.

It was one afternoon, when they were seated in the shade of the airship, cleaning their guns, and discussing the plans they had best follow next, that our travellers suddenly heard a great commotion amongst the Africans, who had for the past hour been very quiet, most of them sleeping after the feasts. They yelled and shouted, and began to beat their drums.

"Something is coming," said Ned.

"Perhaps there's going to be a fight," suggested Tom.

"Maybe it's the red pygmies," said Mr. Damon. "Bless my—"

But what he was going to bless he did not say, for at that instant it seemed as if every native in sight suddenly disappeared, almost like magic. They sank down into the grass, darted into their huts, or hid in the tall grass.

"What can it be?" cried Tom, as he looked to see that his rifle was in working order.

"Some enemy," declared Mr. Anderson.

"There they are!" cried Ned Newton, and as he spoke there burst into view, coming from the tall grass that covered the plain about the village, a herd of savage, wild buffaloes. On rushed the shaggy creatures, their long, sharp horns seeming like waving spears as they advanced.

"Here's more sport!" cried Tom.

"No! Not sport! Danger!" yelled Mr. Durban. "They're headed right for us!"

"Then we'll stop them," declared the young inventor, as he raised his gun.

"No! No!" begged the old hunter. "It's as much as our lives are worth to try to stop a rush of wild buffaloes. You couldn't do it with Gatling guns. We can kill a few, but the rest won't stop until they've finished us and the aeroplane too."

"Then what's to be done?" demanded Mr. Anderson.

"Get into the airship!" cried Mr. Durban. "Send her up. It's the only way to get out of their path. Then we can shoot them from above, and drive them away!"

Quickly the adventurers leaped into the craft. On thundered the buffaloes. Tom feared he could not get the motor started quickly enough. He did not dare risk rising by means of the aeroplane feature, but at once started the gas machine.

The big bag began to fill. Nearer came the wild creatures, thundering over the ground, snorting and bellowing with rage.

"Quick, Tom!" yelled Ned, and at that instant the Black Hawk shot upward, just as the foremost of the buffaloes passed underneath, vainly endeavoring to gore the craft with their sweeping horns. The air-travelers had risen just in time.

"Now it's our turn!" shouted Ned, as he began firing from above into the herd of infuriated animals below him. Tom, after seeing that the motor was working well, sent the airship circling about, while standing in the steering tower, he guided his craft here and there, meanwhile pouring a fusillade of his wireless bullets into the buffaloes. Many of them dropped in their tracks, but the big herd continued to rush here and there, crashing into the frail native huts, tearing them down, and, whenever a black man appeared, chasing after him infuriatedly.

"Keep at it!" cried Mr. Durban, as he poured more lead into the buffaloes. "If we don't kill enough of them, and drive the others away, there won't be anything left of this village."

CHAPTER XVIII

NEWS OF THE RED PYGMIES

Seldom had it been the lot of Tom and his companions to take part in such a novel hunting scene as that in which they were now participating. With the airship moving quickly about, darting here and there under the guidance of the young inventor, the erratic movements hither and thither of the buffaloes could be followed exactly. Wherever the mass of the herd went the airship hovered over them.

"Want any help, Tom?" called Ned, who was firing as fast as his gun could be worked.

"I guess not," answered the steersman of the Black Hawk, who was dividing his attention between managing the craft and firing his electric rifle.

The others, too, were kept busy with their weapons, shooting down on the infuriated animals. It seemed like a needless slaughter, but it was not. Had it not been for the white men, the native village, which consisted of only frail huts, would have been completely wiped out by the animals. As it was they were kept "milling" about in a circle in an open space, just as stampeded cattle on the western ranges are kept from getting away, by being forced round and round.

Not a native was in sight, all being hidden away in the jungle or dense grass. The white hunters in their airship had matters to themselves.

At last the firing proved even too much for the buffaloes which, as we have said, are among the most dreaded of African beasts. With bellows of fear, the leading bulls of the herd unable to find the enemy above their heads, darted off into the forest the way they had come.

"There they go!" yelled Mr. Durban.

"Yes, and I'm glad to see the last of them," added Mr. Anderson, with a breath of relief.

"Score another victory for the electric rifle," exclaimed Ned.

"Oh, you did as much execution as I did," declared the inventor of the weapon.

"Bless my ramrod!" cried Mr. Damon. "I never shot so much in all my life before."

"Yes, there is enough food to last the natives for a week," observed Mr. Durban, as Tom adjusted the deflecting rudder to send the airship down.

"It won't last much longer at the rate they eat," spoke the young inventor with a laugh. "I never saw such fellows for appetites! They seem to eat in their sleep."

There were many dead buffaloes, but there was no fear that the meat, which was much prized by the Africans, would be wasted. Already the natives were coming from their hiding places, knowing that the danger was over. Once more they sang the praises of the mighty white hunters, and the magical air craft in which they moved about.

With the elephants previously killed, the buffaloes provided material for a great feast, preparations for which were at once gotten under way, in spite of the fact that the blacks had hardly stopped eating since the big hunt began. But it was about all they had to do.

Some of the buffaloes were very large, and there were a number of pairs of fine horns. Tom and Ned had some of the blacks cut them off for trophies, and they were stored in the airship together with the ivory.

Becoming rather tired of seeing so much feasting, our friends bade the Africans farewell the next day, and once more resumed their quest. They navigated through the air for another week, stopping at several villages, and scanning the jungles and plains by means of powerful telescopes, for a sight of the red pygmies. They also asked for news of the sacking of the missionary settlement, but, beyond meager facts, could learn nothing.

"Well, we've got to keep on, that's all," decided Mr. Durban. "We may find them most unexpectedly."

"I'm sorry if I have taken you away from your work of gathering ivory," spoke Mr. Anderson. "Perhaps you had better let me go, and I'll see if I can't organize a band of friendly blacks, and search for the red dwarfs myself."

"Not much!" exclaimed Tom warmly. "I said we'd help rescue those missionaries, and we'll do it, too!"

"Of course," declared the old elephant hunter. "We have quite a lot of ivory and, while we need more to make it pay well, we can look for it after we rescue the missionaries as well as before. Perhaps there will be a lot of elephants in the pygmies' land."

"I was only thinking that we can't go on forever in the airship." said Mr. Anderson. "You'll have to go back to civilization soon, won't you, Tom, to get gasolene?"

"No, we have enough for at least a month," answered the young inventor. "I took aboard an unusually large supply when we started."

"What would happen if we ran out of it in the jungle?" asked Ned.

"Bless my pocketbook! What an unpleasant question!" exclaimed Mr. Damon. "You are almost as cheerful, Ned, as was my friend Mr. Parker, the gloomy scientist, who was always predicting dire happenings."

"Well, I was only wondering," said Ned, who was a little abashed by the manner in which his inquiry was received.

"Oh, it would be all right," declared Tom. "We would simply become a balloon, and in time the wind would blow us to some white settlement. There is plenty of material for making the lifting gas."

This was reassuring, and, somewhat easier in mind, Ned took his place in the observation tower which looked down on the jungle over which they were passing.

It was a dense forest. At times there could be seen, in the little clearings, animals darting along. There were numbers of monkeys, an occasional herd of buffaloes were observed, sometimes a solitary stray elephant was noted, and as for birds, there were thousands of them. It was like living over a circus, Ned declared.

They had descended one day just outside a large native village to make inquiries about elephants and the red pygmies. Of the big beasts no signs had been seen in several months, the hunters of the tribe told Mr. Durban. And concerning the red pygmies, the blacks seemed indisposed to talk.

Tom and the others could not understand this, until a witch-doctor, whom the elephant hunter had met some time ago, when he was on a previous expedition, told him that the tribe had a superstitious fear of speaking of the little men.

"They may be around us—in the forest or jungle at any minute," the witch-doctor said. "We never speak of them."

"Say, do you suppose that can be a clew?" asked Tom eagerly. "They may be nearer at hand than we think."

"It's possible." admitted the hunter. "Suppose we stay here for a few days, and I'll see if I can't get some of the natives to go off scouting in the woods, and locate them, or at least put us on the trail of the red dwarfs."

This was considered good advice, and it was decided to adopt it. Accordingly the airship was put in a safe place, and our friends prepared to spend a week, if necessary, in the native village. Their presence with the wonderful craft was a source of wonder, and by means of some trinkets judiciously given to the native king, and also to his head subjects, and to the witch-doctors (who were a power in the land), the good opinion of the tribe was won. Then, by promising rewards to some of the bolder hunters, Mr. Durban finally succeeded in getting them to go off scouting in the jungle for a clew to the red pygmies.

"Now we'll have to wait," said Mr. Anderson, "and I hope we get good news."

Our friends spent their time observing some of the curious customs of the natives, and in witnessing some odd dances gotten up in their honor. They also went hunting, and got plenty of game, for which their hosts were duly grateful. Tom did some night stalking and found his illuminating bullets a great success.

One hot afternoon Tom and Mr. Damon strolled off a little way into the jungle, Tom with his electric weapon, in case he saw any game. But no animals save a few big monkeys where to be seen, and the young inventor scorned to kill them. It seemed too much like firing at a human being he said, though the natives stated that some of the baboons and apes were fierce, and would attack one on the slightest provocation.

"I believe I'll sit down here and rest," said Tom, after a mile's tramp, as he came to a little clearing in the woods.

"Very well, I'll go on," decided Mr. Damon. "Mr. Durban said there were sometimes rare orchids in these jungles, and I am very fond of those odd flowers. I'm going to see if I can get any."

He disappeared behind a fringe of moss-grown trees, and Tom sat down, with his rifle across his knees. He was thinking of many things, but chiefly of what yet lay before them—the discovery of the red dwarfs and the possible rescue of the missionaries.

He might have been thus day-dreaming for perhaps a half hour, when he suddenly heard great commotion in the jungle, in the direction in which Mr. Damon had vanished. It sounded as though some one was running rapidly. Then came the report of the odd man's gun.

"He's seen some game!" exclaimed Tom, jumping up, and preparing to follow his friend. But he did not have the chance. An instant later Mr. Damon burst through the bushes with every appearance of fright, his gun held above his head with one hand, and his pith helmet swaying to and fro in the other.

"They're coming!" he cried to Tom.

"Who, the red pygmies?"

"No, but a couple of rhinoceroses are after me. I wounded one, and he and his mate are right behind. Don't let them catch me, Tom!"

Mr. Damon was very much alarmed, and there was good occasion for it, as Tom saw a moment later, for two fierce rhinoceroses burst out of the jungle almost on the heels of the fleeing man.

Thought was not quicker than Tom Swift. He raised his deadly rifle, and pressed the button. A charge of wireless electricity shot toward the foremost animal, and it was dropped in its tracks. The other came on woofing and snorting with rage. It was the one Mr. Damon had slightly wounded.

"Come on!" yelled the young inventor, for his friend was in front of the beast, and in range with the rifle. "Jump to one side, Mr. Damon."

Mr. Damon tried, but his foot slipped, and there was no need for jumping. He fell and rolled over. The rhinoceros swerved toward him, with the probable intention of goring the prostrate man with the formidable horn, but it had no chance. Once more the young inventor fired, this time with a heavier charge, and the animal instantly toppled over dead.

"Are you hurt?" asked Tom anxiously, as he ran to his friend. Mr. Damon got up slowly. He felt all over himself, and then answered:

"No, Tom, I guess I'm not hurt, except in my dignity. Never again will I fire at a sleeping rhinoceros unless you are with me. I had a narrow escape," and he shook Tom's hand heartily.

"Did you see any orchids?" asked the lad with a smile.

"No, those beasts didn't give me a chance! Bless my tape measure! but they're big fellows!"

Indeed they were fine specimens, and there was the usual rejoicing among the natives when they brought in the great bodies, pulling them to the village with ropes made of vines.

After this Mr. Damon was careful not to go into the jungle alone, nor, in fact, did any of our friends so venture. Mr. Durban said it was not safe.

They remained a full week in the native village, and received no news. In fact, all but one of the hunters came back to report that there was no sign of the red pygmies in that neighborhood.

"Well, I guess we might as well move on, and see what we can do ourselves," said Mr. Durban.

"Let's wait until the last hunter comes back," suggested Tom. "He may bring word."

"Some of his friends think he'll never come back," remarked Mr. Anderson.

"Why not?" asked Ned.

"They think he has been killed by some wild beast."

But this fear was ungrounded. It was on the second day after the killing of the rhinoceroses that, as Tom was tinkering away in the engine-room of the airship, and thinking that perhaps they had better get under way, that a loud shouting was heard among the natives.

"I wonder what's up now?" mused the young inventor as he went outside. He saw Mr. Durban and Mr. Anderson running toward the ship. Behind them was a throng of blacks, led by a weary man whom Tom recognized as the missing hunter. The lad's heart beat high with hope. Did the African bring news?

On came Mr. Durban, waving his hands to Tom.

"We've located 'em!" he shouted.

"Not the red pygmies?" asked Tom eagerly.

"Yes; this hunter has news of them. He has been to the border of their country, and narrowly escaped capture. Then he was attacked by a lion, and slightly wounded. But, Tom, now we can get on the trail!"

"Good!" cried the young inventor. "That's fine news!" and he rejoiced that once more there would be activity, for he was tired of remaining in the African camp, and then, too, he wanted to proceed to the rescue. Already it might be too late to save the unfortunate missionaries.

CHAPTER XIX

AN APPEAL FOR HELP

The African hunter's story was soon told. He had gone on farther than had any of his companions, and, being a bold and brave man, had penetrated into the very fastness of the jungle where few would dare to venture.

But even he had despaired of getting on the trail of the fierce little red men, until one afternoon, just at dusk he had heard voices in the forest. Crouching behind a fallen tree, he waited and saw passing by some of the pygmy hunters, armed with bows and arrows, and blowguns. They had been out after game. Cautiously the hunter followed them, until he located one of their odd villages, which consisted of little mud huts, poorly made.

The black hunter remained in the vicinity of the pygmies all that night, and was almost caught, for some wild dogs which hung around the village smelled him out, and attracted to him the attention of the dwarf savages. The hunter took to a tree, and so escaped. Then, carefully marking the trail, he came away in the morning. When near home, a lion had attacked him, but he speared the beast to death, after a hand-to-hand struggle in which his leg was torn.

"And do you think we can find the place?" asked Ned, when Mr. Durban had finished translating the hunter's story.

"I think so," was the reply.

"But is this the settlement where the missionaries are?" asked Tom anxiously.

"That is what we don't know," said Mr. Anderson. "The native scout could not learn that. But once we get on the trail of the dwarfs, I think we can easily find the particular tribe which has the captives."

"At any rate, we'll get started and do something," declared Tom, and the next day, after the African hunter had described, as well as he could, where the place was, the Black Hawk was sent up into the air, good-bys were called down, and once more the adventurers were under way.

It was decided that they had better proceed cautiously, and lower the airship, and anchor it, sometime before getting above the place where the pygmy village was.

"For they may see us, and, though they don't know what our craft is, they may take the alarm and hide deeper in the jungle with the prisoners, where we can't find them," said Tom.

His plan was adopted, and, while it had taken the native hunter several days to reach the borders of the dwarfs' land, those in the airship made the trip in one day. That is, they came as far toward it as they thought would be safe, and one night, having located a landmark which Mr. Durban said was on the border, the nose of the Black Hawk was pointed downward, and soon they were encamped in a little clearing in the midst of the dense jungle which was all about them.

With his electric rifle, Tom noiselessly killed some birds, very much like chicken, of which an excellent meal was made and then, as it became dark very early, and as nothing could be done, they lighted a campfire, and retired inside their craft to pass the night.

It must have been about midnight that Tom, who was a light sleeper at times, was awakened by some noise outside the window near which his stateroom was. He sat up and listened, putting out his hand to where his rifle stood in the corner near his bunk. The lad heard stealthy footsteps pattering about on the deck of the airship. There was a soft, shuffling sound, such as a lion or a tiger makes, when walking on bare boards. In spite of himself, Tom felt the hair on his head beginning to creep, and a shiver ran down his back.

"There's something out there!" he whispered. "I wonder if I'd better awaken the others? No, if it's a sneaking lion, I can manage to kill him, but—"

He paused as another suggestion came to him.

The red pygmies! They went barefoot! Perhaps they were swarming about the ship which they might have discovered in the darkness.

Tom Swift's heart beat rapidly. He got softly out of his bunk, and, with his rifle in hand made his way to the door opening on deck. On his way he gently awakened Ned and Mr. Durban, and whispered to them his fear.

"If the red pygmies are out there we'll need all our force," said the old elephant hunter. "Call Mr. Damon and Mr. Anderson, Ned, and tell them to bring their guns."

Soon they were all ready, fully armed. They listened intently. The airship was all in darkness, for lights drew a horde of insects. The campfire had died down. The soft footsteps could still be heard moving about the deck.

"That sounds like only one person or animal," whispered Ned.

"It does," agreed Tom. "Wait a minute, I'll fire an illuminating charge, and we can see what it is."

The others posted themselves at windows that gave a view of the deck. Tom poked his electric rifle out of a crack of the door, and shot forth into the darkness one of the blue illuminations. The deck of the craft was instantly lighted up brilliantly, and in the glare, crouched on the deck, could be seen a powerful black man, nearly naked, gazing at the hunters.

"A black!" gasped Tom, as the light died out. "Maybe it is one from the village we just left. What do you want? Who are you?" called the lad, forgetting that the Africans spoke only their own language. To the surprise of all, there came his reply in broken English:

"Me Tomba! Me go fo' help for Missy Illingway—fo' Massy Illingway. Me run away from little red men! Me Christian black man. Oh, if you be English, help Missy Illingway—she most die! Please help. Tomba go but Tomba be lost! Please help!"

CHAPTER XX

THE FIGHT

Surprise, for the moment, held Tom and the others speechless. To be answered in English, poor and broken as it was, by a native African, was strange enough, but when this same African was found aboard the airship, in the midst of the jungle, at midnight, it almost passed the bounds of possibility.

"Tomba!" mused Tom, wondering where he had heard that name before. "Tomba?"

"Of course!" cried Mr. Anderson, suddenly. "Don't you remember? That's the name of the servant of Mr. and Mrs. Illingway, who escaped and brought news of their capture by the pygmies. That's who Tomba is."

"Yes, but Tomba escaped," objected Mr. Durban. "He went to the white settlements with the news. How comes he here?"

"We'll have to find out," said Tom, simply. "Tomba, are you there?" he called, as he fired another illuminating charge. It disclosed the black man standing up on the deck, and looking at them appealingly.

"Yes, Tomba here," was the answer. "Oh, you be English, Tomba know. Please help Missy and Massy Illingway. Red devils goin' kill 'em pretty much quick."

"Come in!" called Tom, as he turned on the electric lights in the airship. "Come in and tell us all about it. But how did you get here?"

"Maybe there are two Tombas," suggested Ned.

"Bless my safety razor!" cried Mr. Damon "perhaps Ned is right!"

But he wasn't, as they learned when they had questioned the African, who came inside the airship, looking wonderingly around at the many strange things he saw. He was the same Tomba who had escaped the massacre, and had taken news of the capture of his master and mistress to the white settlement. In vain after that he had tried to organize a band to go back with him to the rescue, but the whites in the settlement were too few, and the natives too timid. Then Tomba, with grief in his heart, and not wanting to live while the missionaries whom he had come to care for very much, were captives, he went back into the jungle, determined, if he could not help them, that at least he would share their fate, and endeavor to be of some service to them in their captivity.

After almost unbelievable hardships, he had found the red pygmies, and had allowed himself to be captured by them. They rejoiced greatly in the possession of the big black man, and for some strange reason had not killed him. He was allowed to share the captivity of his master and mistress.

Time went on, and the pygmies did not kill their prisoners. They even treated them with some kindness but were going to sacrifice them at their great annual festival, which was soon to take place. Mr. and Mrs. Illingway, Tomba told our friends in his broken English, had urged him to escape at the first opportunity. They knew if he could get away he would travel through the jungle. They could not, even if they had not been so closely guarded that escape was out of the question.

But Tomba refused to go until Mr. Illingway had said that perhaps he might get word to some white hunters, and so send help to the captives. This Tomba consented to do, and, watching his chance, he did escape. That was several nights ago, and he had been traveling through the jungle ever since. It was by mere accident that he came upon the anchored airship, and his curiosity led him to board her. The rest is known.

"Well, of all queer yarns, this is the limit!" exclaimed Tom, when the black had finished. "What had we better do about it?"

"Get ready to attack the red pygmies at once!" decided Mr. Durban. "If we wait any longer it may be too late!"

"My idea, exactly," declared Mr. Anderson.

"Bless my bowie-knife!" cried Mr. Damon. "I'd like to get a chance at the red imps! Come on, Tom! Let's start at once."

"No, we need daylight to fight by," replied Tom, with a smile at his friend's enthusiasm. "We'll go forward in the morning."

"In the airship?" asked Mr. Damon.

"I think so," answered Tom. "There can be no advantage now in trying to conceal ourselves. We can move upon them from where we are so quickly that they won't have much chance to get away. Besides it will take us too long to make our way through the jungle afoot. For, now that the escape of Tomba must be known, they may kill the captives at once to forestall any rescue."

"Then we'll move forward in the morning," declared Mr. Durban.

They took Tomba with them in the airship the next day, though he prayed fervently before he consented to it. But they needed him to point out the exact location of the pygmies' village, since it was not the one the hunter-scout had been near.

The Black Hawk sailed through the air. On board eager eyes looked down for a first sight of the red imps. Tomba, who was at Tom's side in the steering tower, told him, as best he could, from time to time, how to set the rudders.

"Pretty soon by-em-by be there," said the black man at length. "Pass ober dat hill, den red devils live."

"Well, we'll soon be over that hill," announced Tom grimly. "I guess we'd better get our rifles ready for the battle."

"Are you going to attack them at once?" asked Mr. Damon.

"Well," answered the young inventor, "I don't believe we ought to kill any of them if we can avoid it. I don't like to do such a thing but, perhaps we can't help ourselves. My plan is to take the airship down, close to the hut where the missionaries are confined. Tomba can point it out to us. If we can rescue them without bloodshed, so much the better. But we'll fight if we have to."

Grimly they watched as the airship sailed over the hill. Then suddenly there came into view a collection of mud huts on a vast plain, surrounded by dense jungle on every side. As the travelers looked, they could see little creatures running wildly about. Even without a glass it could be noted that their bodies were covered with a curious growth of thick sandy hair.

"The red pygmies!" cried Tom. "Now for the rescue!"

Eagerly Tomba indicated the hut where his master and mistress were held. Telling his friends to have their weapons in readiness, Tom steered the airship toward the rude shelter whence he hoped to take the missionaries. Down to the ground swiftly shot the Black Hawk. Tom checked her with a quick movement of the deflecting rudder, and she landed gently on the wheels.

"Mr. Illingway! Mrs. Illingway! We have come to rescue you!" yelled the young inventor, as he stepped out on the deck, with his electric rifle in his hand. "Where are you? Can you come out?"

The door of the hut was burst open, and a white man and woman, recognizable as such, even in the rude skins that clothed them, rushed out. Wonder spread over their faces as they saw the great airship. They dropped on their knees.

The next instant a swarm of savage little red men surrounded them, and rudely bore them, strugglingly, back into the hut.

"Come on!" cried Tom, about to leap to the ground. "It's now or never! We must save them!"

Mr. Durban pulled him back, and pointed to a horde of the red-haired savages rushing toward the airship. "They'd tear you to pieces in a minute!" cried the old hunter. "We must fight them from the ship."

There was a curious whistling sound in the air. Mr. Durban looked up.

"Duck, everybody!" he yelled. "They're firing arrows at us! Get under shelter, for they may be poisoned!"

Tom and the others darted into the craft. The arrows rattled on deck in a shower, and hundreds of the red imps were rushing up to give battle. Inside the hut where the missionaries were, it was now quiet. Tom Swift wondered if they still lived.

"Give 'em as good as they send!" cried Mr. Durban. "We will have to fire at them now. Open up with your electric rifle, Tom!"

As he spoke the elephant hunter fired into the midst of the screaming savages. The battle had begun.

CHAPTER XXI

DRIVEN BACK

What the travelers had heard regarding the fierceness and courage of the red pygmies had not been one bit exaggerated. Never had such desperate fighting ever taken place. The red dwarfs, scarcely one of whom was more than three feet high, were strongly built, and there were so many of them, and they battled together with such singleness of purpose, that they were more formidable than a tribe of ordinary- sized savages would have been.

And their purpose was to utterly annihilate the enemy that had so unexpectedly come upon them. It did not matter to them that Tom and the others had arrived in an airship. The strange craft had no superstitious terror for them, as it had for the simpler blacks.

"Bless my multiplication tables!" cried Mr. Damon. "What a mob of them!"

"Almost too many!" murmured Tom Swift, who was rapidly firing his electric rifle at them. "We can never hope to drive them back, I'm afraid."

Indeed from every side of the plain, and even from the depths of the jungle the red dwarfs were now pouring. They yelled most horribly, screaming in rage, brandishing their spears and clubs, and keeping up an incessant fire of big arrows from their bows, and smaller ones from the blowguns.

As yet none of our friends had been hit, for they were sheltered in the airship, and as the windows were covered with a mesh of wire, to keep out insects, this also served to prevent the arrows from entering. There were loopholes purposely made to allow the rifles to be thrust out.

Mercifully, Tom and the others fired only to disable, and not to kill the red pygmies. Wounded in the arms or legs, the little savages would be incapable of fighting, and this plan was followed. But so fierce were they that some, who were wounded twice, still kept up the attack.

Tom's electric rifle was well adapted for this work, as he could regulate the charge to merely stun, no matter at what part of the body it was directed. So he could fire indiscriminantly, whereas the others had to aim carefully. And Tom's fire was most effective. He disabled scores of the red imps, but scores of others sprang up to take their places.

After their first rush the pygmies had fallen back before the well- directed fire of our friends, but as their chiefs and head men urged them to the attack again, they came back with still fiercer energy. Some, more bold than the others, even leaped to the deck of the airship, and tried to tear the screens from the windows. They partly succeeded, and in one casement from which Ned was firing they made a hole.

Into this they shot a flight of arrows, and one slightly wounded the bank clerk on the arm. The wound was at once treated with antiseptics, after the window had been barricaded, and Ned declared that he was ready to renew the fight. Tom, too, got an arrow scratch on the neck, and one of the barbs entered Mr. Durban's leg, but the sturdy elephant hunter would not give up, and took his place again after the wound had been bandaged.

From time to time as he worked his electric gun, which had been charged to its utmost capacity, Tom glanced at the hut where the missionaries were prisoners. There was no movement noticed about it, and no sound came from it. Tom wondered what had happened inside—he wondered what was happening as the battle progressed.

Fiercely the fight was kept up. Now the red imps would be driven back, and again they would swarm about the airship, until it seemed as if they must overwhelm it. Then the fire of the white adventurers was redoubled. The electric rifle did great work, and Tom did not have to stop and refill the magazine, as did the others.

Suddenly, above the noise of the conflict, Tom Swift heard an ominous sound. It was a hissing in the air, and well he knew what it was.

"The gas bag!" he cried. "They've punctured it! The vapor is escaping. If they put too many holes in the bag it will be all up with us!"

"What's to be done?" asked Mr. Durban.

"If we can't drive them back we must retreat ourselves!" declared Tom desperately. "Our only hope is to keep the airship safe from harm."

Once more came a rush of the savages. They had discovered that the gas bag was vulnerable, and were directing their arrows against that. It was punctured in several more places. The gas was rapidly escaping.

"We've got to retreat!" yelled Tom. He hurried to the engine-room, and turned on the power. The great propellers revolved, and sent the Black Hawk scudding across the level plain. With yells of surprise the red dwarfs scattered and made way for it.

Up into the air it mounted on the broad wings. For the time being our friends has been driven back, and the missionaries whom they had come to rescue were still in the hands of the savages.

CHAPTER XXII

A NIGHT ATTACK

"Well, what's to be done?"

Tom Swift asked that question.

"Bless my percussion cap! They certainly are the very worst imps for fighting that I ever heard of," commented Mr. Damon helplessly.

"Is the gas bag much punctured?" asked Ned Newton.

"Wait a minute," resumed the young inventor, as he pulled the speed lever a trifle farther over, thereby sending the craft forward more swiftly, "I think my question ought to be answered first. What's to be done? Are we going to run away, and leave that man and woman to their fate?"

"Of course not!" declared Mr. Durban stoutly, "but we couldn't stay there, and have them destroy the airship."

"No, that's so," admitted Tom, "if we lost the airship it would be all up with us and our chances of rescuing the missionaries. But what can we do? I hate to retreat!"

"But what else is there left for us?" demanded Ned.

"Nothing, of course. But we've got to plan to get the best of those red pygmies. We can't go back in the airship, and give them open battle. There are too many of them, and, by Jove! I believe more are coming every minute!"

Tom and the others looked down. From all sides of the plain, hastening toward the village of mud huts, from which our friends were retreating, could be seen swarms of the small but fierce savages. They were coming from the jungle, and were armed with war clubs, bows and arrows and the small but formidable blowguns.

"Where are they coming from?" asked Mr. Damon.

"From the surrounding tribes," explained Mr. Durban. "They have been summoned to do battle against us."

"But how did the ones we fought get word to the others so soon?" Ned demanded.

"Oh, they have ways of signaling," explained Mr. Anderson. "They can make the notes of some of their hollow-tree drums carry a long distance, and then they are very swift runners, and can penetrate into the jungle along paths that a white man would hardly see. They also use the smoke column as a signal, as our own American Indians used to do. Oh, they can summon all their tribesmen to the fight, and they probably will. Likely the sound of our guns attracted the imps, though if we all had electric rifles like Tom's they wouldn't make any noise."

"Well, my rifle didn't appear to do so very much good this time," observed the young inventor, as he stopped the forward motion of the ship now, and let it hover over the plain in sight of the village, the gas bag serving to sustain the craft, and there was little wind to cause it to drift. "Those fellows didn't seem to mind being hurt and killed any more than if mosquitoes were biting them."

"The trouble is we need a whole army, armed with electric rifles to make a successful attack," said Mr. Durban. "There are swarms of them there now, and more coming every minute. I do hope Mr. and Mrs. Illingway are alive yet."

"Yes," added Mr. Anderson solemnly, "we must hope for the best. But, like Tom Swift, I ask, what's to be done?"

"Bless my thinking cap!" exclaimed Mr. Damon. "It seems to me if we can't fight them openly in the daytime, there's only one other thing to do."

"What's that?" asked Tom. "Go away? I'll not do it!"

"No, not go away," exclaimed Mr. Damon, "but make a night attack. We ought to be able to do something then, and with your illuminating rifle, Tom, we'd have an advantage! What do you say?"

"I say it's the very thing!" declared Tom, with sudden enthusiasm. "We'll attack them to-night, when they're off their guard, and we'll see if we can't get the missionaries out of that hut. And to better fool the savages, we'll just disappear now, and make 'em believe we've flown away."

"Then the missionaries will think we're deserting them," objected Mr. Anderson.

But there was no help for it, and so Tom once more turned on the power and the craft sailed away.

Tomba, the faithful black, begged to be allowed to go down, and tell his master and mistress that help would soon be at hand again, even though it looked like a retreat on the part of the rescuers, but this could not be permitted.

"They'd tear you in pieces as soon as you got among those red imps," said Tom. "You stay here, Tomba, and you can help us to-night."

"A'right, me glad help lick red fellows," said the black, with as cheerful a grin as he could summon.

The Black Hawk circled around, with Tom and the others looking for a good place to land. They were out of sight of the village now but did not doubt but that they were observed by the keen eyes of the little men.

"We want to pick out a place where they won't come upon us as we descend," declared Tom. "We've got to mend some leaks in the gas bag, for, while they are not serious, if we get any more punctures they may become so. So we've got to pick out a good place to go down."

Finally, by means of powerful glasses, a desolate part of the jungle was selected. No files of the red dwarfs, coming from their scattered villages to join their tribesmen, had been noted in the vicinity picked out, and it was hoped that it would answer. Slowly the airship settled to earth, coming to rest in a thick grove of trees, where there was an opening just large enough to allow the Black Hawk to enter.

Our friends were soon busy repairing the leaks in the bag, while Mr. Damon got a meal ready. As they ate they talked over plans for the night attack.

It was decided to wait until it was about two o'clock in the morning, as at that hour the dwarfs were most generally asleep, Tomba said. They always stayed up quite late, sitting around camp-fires, and eating the meat which the hunters brought in each day. But their carousings generally ended at midnight, the black said, and then they fell into a heavy sleep. They did not post guards, but since they knew of the presence of the white men in the airship, they might do it this time.

"Well, we've got to take our chance," decided Tom. "We'll start off from here about one o'clock, and I'll send the ship slowly along. We'll get right over the hut where the captives are, if possible, and then descend. I'll manage the ship, and one of you can work the electric rifle if they attack us. We'll make a dash, get Mr. and Mrs. Illingway from the hut, and make a quick get-away."

It sounded good, and they were impatient to put it into operation. That afternoon Tom and his friends went carefully over every inch of their craft, to repair it and have it in perfect working order. Guns were cleaned, and plenty of ammunition laid out. Then, shortly after one o'clock in the morning the ship was sent up, and with the searchlight ready to be turned on instantly, and with his electric rifle near at hand, Tom Swift guided his craft on to the attack. Soon they could see the glow of dying fires in the dwarfs' village, but no sound came from the sleeping hordes of red imps.

CHAPTER XXIII

THE RESCUE

"Can you make out the hut, Tom?" asked Ned, as he stood at his chum's side in the steering tower, and gazed downward on the silent village.

"Not very clearly. Suppose you take a look through the night- glasses. Maybe you'll have better luck."

Ned peered long and earnestly.

"No, I can't see a thing." he said. "It all looks to be a confused jumble of huts. I can't tell one from the other. We'll have to go lower."

"I don't want to do that," objected Tom. "If this attack succeeds at all, it will have to be sharp and quick. If we go down where they can spot us, and work our way up to the hut where the captives are, we'll run the chance of an attack that may put us out of business."

"Yes, we ought to get right over the hut, and then make a sudden swoop down," admitted Ned, "but if we can't see it—"

"I have it!" cried Tom suddenly. "Tomba! That African can see in the dark like a cat. Why, just before we started I dropped a wrench, and I didn't have any matches handy to look for it. I was groping around in the dark trying to get my hands on it, and you know it was pretty black in the jungle. Well, along come Tomba. And he spotted it at once and picked it up. We'll call him here and get him to point out the hut. He can tell me how to steer."

"Good!" cried Ned, and the black was soon standing in the pilot house. He comprehended what was wanted of him, and peered down, seeking to penetrate the darkness.

"Shall I go down a little lower?" asked Tom.

For a moment Tomba did not answer. Then he uttered an exclamation of pleasure.

"Me see hut!" he said, clutching Tom's arm. "Down dere!" He pointed, but neither Tom nor Ned could see it. However, as Tomba was now giving directions, telling Tom when to go to the left or the right, as the wind currents deflected they were certain of soon reaching the place where Mr. and Mrs. Illingway were concealed, if they were still alive.

The Black Hawk was moving slowly, and was not under as good control as if she had been making ninety miles an hour. As it was desired to proceed as quietly as possible, the craft was being used as a dirigible balloon, and the propellers were whirled around by means of a small motor, worked by a storage battery. While not much power was obtained this way, there was the advantage of silence, which was very necessary. Slowly the Black Hawk sailed on through the night. In silence the adventurers waited for the moment of action. They had their weapons in readiness. Mr. Durban was to work the electric rifle, as all Tom's attention would be needed at the machinery. As soon as the craft had made a landing he was to leap out, carrying a revolver in either hand, and, followed by Tomba, would endeavor to gain entrance to the hut, break through the flimsy grass-woven curtain over the doorway, and get Mr. and Mrs. Illingway out. Ned, Mr. Damon and the other two men would stand by to fire on the red pygmies as soon as they commenced the attack, which they would undoubtedly do as soon as the guards of the captives raised the alarm.

The airship was in darkness, for it would have been dangerous to show a light. Some wakeful dwarf might see the moving illumination in the sky, and raise a cry.

"Mos' dere," announced Tomba at length. And then, for the first time, Ned and Tom had a glimpse of the hut. It stood away from the others, and was easy to pick out in daylight, but even the darkness offered no handicap to Tomba. "Right over him now," he suddenly called, as he leaned out of the pilot house window, and looked down. "Right over place. Oh, Tomba glad when he see Missy an' Massy!"

"Yes, I hope you do see them," murmured Tom, as he pulled the lever which would pump the gas from the inflated bag, and compress it into tanks, until it was needed again to make the ship rise. Slowly the Black Hawk sank down.

"Get ready!" called Tom in a low voice.

It was a tense moment. Every one of the adventurers felt it, and all but Tom grasped their weapons with tighter grips. They were ready to spring out as soon as a landing was made. Tom managed the machinery in the dark, for he knew every wheel, gear and lever, and could have put his hand on any one with his eyes shut. The two loaded revolvers were on a shelf in front of him. The side door of the pilot house was ajar, to allow him quick egress.

Tomba, armed with a big club he had picked up in the jungle, was ready to follow. The black was eager for the fray to begin, though how he and the others would fare amid the savages was hard to say.

Still not a sound broke the quiet. It was very dark, for nearly all the camp fires, over which the nightly feast had been prepared, were out. The hut could be dimly made out, however.

Suddenly there was a slight tremor through the ship. She seemed to shiver, and bound upward a little.

"We've landed!" whispered Tom. "Now for it! Come on, Tomba!"

The big black glided after the lad like a shadow. With his two weapons held in readiness our hero went out on deck. The others, with cocked rifles, stood ready for the attack to open. It had been decided that as soon as the first alarm was given by the dwarfs, which would probably be when Tom broke into the hut, the firing would begin.

"Open!" called Tom to Tomba, and the big black dashed his club through the grass curtain over the doorway of the hut. He fairly leaped inside, with a cry of battle on his lips.

"Mr. Illingway! Mrs. Illingway!" called Tom, "We've come to save you. Hurry out. The airship is just outside!"

He fired one shot through the roof of the hut, so that the flash would reveal to him whether or not the two missionaries were in the place. He saw two forms rise up in front of him, and knew that they were the white captives he had observed daring the former attack.

"Oh, what is it?" he heard the woman ask.

"A rescue! Thank the dear Lord!" answered her husband fervently. "Oh, whoever you are, God bless you!"

"Come quickly!" cried Tom, "we haven't a moment to lose!"

He was speaking to absolute blackness now, for it was darker immediately following the revolver flash than before. But he felt a man's hand thrust about his arm, and he knew it was Mr. Illingway.

"Take your wife's hand, and follow me," ordered Tom. "Come, Tomba! Are there any of the red pygmies in here?"

He had not seen any at the weapon's flash, but his question was answered a moment later, for there arose from within and without the hut a chorus of wild yells. At the same time Tom felt small arms grasp him about the legs.

"Come on!" he yelled. "They're awake and after us!"

The din outside increased. Tom heard the rifles of his friends crack. He saw, through the torn door curtain, the flashes of fire. Then came a blue glare, and Tom knew that Mr. Durban was using the electric weapon.

By these intermittent gleams Tom managed to see sufficiently to thrust Mr. and Mrs. Illingway ahead of him. Tomba was at their side. The yells inside the hut were almost deafening. All the red dwarfs left to guard the captives had awakened, and they could see well enough to attack Tom. Fortunately they had no weapons, but they fairly threw themselves upon the sturdy lad, trying to pull him down.

"Go on! Go on!" he yelled to the captives, fairly pushing them along. Then, knowing they were out of the way, he turned and fired his two revolvers as fast as he could pull the triggers, into the very faces of the red imps who were seeking to drag him down. Again and again he fired, until he had emptied both cylinders of his weapons.

He felt the grasps of the fiendish little men relax one by one. Tom finally dragged himself loose, and staggered out of the hut. The captives and Tomba were right in front of him. At the airship, which loomed up in the flashes from the guns and electric rifle, Tom's friends were giving battle. About them swarmed the hordes of savages, with more of the imps pouring in every moment.

"Get aboard!" cried Tom to the missionaries. "Get on the airship, and we'll move out of this!"

He felt a stinging pain in his neck, where an arrow struck him. He tore the arrow out, and rushed forward. Fairly pushing Mr. and Mrs. Illingway up on deck before him, Tom followed. Tomba was capering about his master and mistress, and he swung his big club savagely. He had not been idle, and many a red imp had gone down under his blows.

"Rescued! Rescued!" murmured Mr. Illingway, as Tom hastened to the pilot house to start the motor.

CHAPTER XXIV

TWO OTHER CAPTIVES

But the rescue was not yet accomplished. Those on the airship were still in danger, and grave peril, for all about them were the red savages, shouting, howling, yelling and capering about, as they were now thoroughly aroused, and realized that their captives had been taken away from them. They determined to get them back, and were rallying desperately to battle. Nearly all of them were armed by this time, and flight after flight of spears and arrows were thrown or shot toward the airship.

Fortunately it was too dark to enable the pygmies to take good aim. They were guided, to an extent, by the flashes of fire from the rifles, but these were only momentary. Still some of our friends received slight wounds, for they stood on the open deck of the craft.

"Bless my eye-glasses!" suddenly exclaimed Mr. Damon. "I'm stuck!"

"Don't mind that!" advised Ned. "Keep on pouring lead into them. We'll soon be away from here!"

"Don't fire any more!" called Mr. Durban. "The gun-flashes tell them where to shoot. I'll use the electric rifle. It's better."

They followed his advice, and put aside their weapons. By means of the electric flash, which he projected into the midst of the savages, without the glare coming on the airship, Mr. Durban was able to tell where to aim. Once he had a mass of red pygmies located, he could keep on shooting charge after charge into their midst.

"Use it full power!" called Tom, as he opened the gas machine to its widest capacity, so the bag would quickly fill, and the craft be sent forward, for it was so dark, and the ground near the huts so uneven, that the Black Hawk could not rise as an aeroplane.

The elephant hunter turned on full strength in the electric gun and the wireless bullets were sent into the midst of the attackers. The result was surprising. They were so closely packed together that when one was hit the electrical shock was sent through his nearly naked body into the naked bodies of his tribesmen who pressed on every side of him. In consequence whole rows of the savages went down at a time, disabled from fighting any more.

Meanwhile Tom was working frantically to hasten the rising of the airship. His neck pained him very much where the arrow had struck him, but he dared not stop now to dress the wound. He could feel the blood running down his side, but he shut his teeth grimly and said nothing.

The two missionaries, scarcely able to believe that they were to be saved, had been shown into an inner cabin by Tomba, who had become somewhat used to the airship by this time, and who could find his way about well in the dark, for no lights had yet been turned on.

Hundreds of pygmies had been disabled, yet still others came to take their places. The gas bag was again punctured in several places, but the rents were small, and Tom knew that he could make the gas faster than it could escape, unless the bag was ripped open.

"They're climbing up the sides!" suddenly called Ned Newton, for he saw several of the little men clambering up. "What shall we do?"

"Pound their fingers!" called Mr. Anderson. "Get clubs and whack them!" It was good advice. Ned remembered on one occasion when he and Tom were looking at Andy Foger's airship, how this method had been proposed when the bank clerk hung on the back fence. As he grabbed up a stick, and proceeded to pound the hands and bare arms of the savages who were clinging to the railing, Ned found himself wondering what had become of the bully. He was to see Andy sooner than he expected.

Suddenly in the midst of the fighting, which was now a hand-to-hand conflict, there was a tremor throughout the length of the airship.

"She's going up!" yelled Ned.

"Bless my check-book!" cried Mr. Damon, "if we don't look out some of these red imps will go up with us, too!"

As he spoke he whacked vigorously at the hands of several of the pygmies, who dropped off with howls of anguish.

The craft quickly shot upward. There were yells of terror from a few of the red savages who remained clinging to different parts of the Black Hawk and then, fearing they might be taken to the clouds, they, too, dropped off. The rescuers and rescued mounted higher and higher, and, when they were far enough up so that there was no danger from the spears or arrows, Tom switched on the lights, and turned the electric current into the search-lantern, the rays of which beamed down on the mass of yelling and baffled savages below.

"A few shots for them to remember us by!" cried Mr. Durban, as he sent more of the paralyzing electric currents into the red imps. Their yell of rage had now turned to shouts of terror, for the gleaming beam of light frightened them more than did the airship, or the bullets of the white men. The red pygmies fled to their huts.

"I guess we gave them a lesson," remarked Tom, as he started the propellers and sent the ship on through the night.

"Why, Tom! You're hurt!" cried Ned, who came into the pilot house at that moment, and saw blood on his chum.

"Only a scratch," the young inventor declared.

"It's more than that," said Mr. Durban who looked at it a little later. "It must be bound up, Tom."

And, while Ned steered the ship back to the jungle clearing whence they had come to make the night attack, Tom's wound was dressed.

Meanwhile the two missionaries had been well taken care of. They were given other garments, even some dresses being provided for Mrs. Illingway, for when the voyage was begun Tom had considered the possibility of having a woman on board, and had bought some ladies' garments. Then, having cast down to earth the ill-smelling skins which formed their clothes while captives, Mr. and Mrs. Illingway, decently dressed, thanked Tom and the others over and over again.

"We had almost given up hope," said the lady, "when we saw them drive you back after the first attack. Oh, it is wonderful to think how you saved us, and in an airship!" and she and her husband began their thanks over again.

A good meal was prepared by Mr. Damon, for the rescuers and rescued ones were hungry, and since they had been held prisoners the two missionaries had not been given very good food.

"Oh, it hardly seems possible that we are eating with white men again," said Mr. Illingway, as he took a second cup of coffee, "hardly possible!"

"And to see electric lights, instead of a camp-fire," added his wife. "What a wonderful airship you have, Tom Swift."

"Yes, it's pretty good," he admitted. "It came in useful to-night, all right."

They were now far enough from the savages, and the pygmies' fires, which had been set aglow anew when the attack began, could no longer be observed.

"We'll land at the place where we camped before," said Tom, who had again assumed charge of the ship, "and in the morning we'll start for civilization."

"No can get two other white men?" suddenly asked Tomba, who had been sitting, gazing at his recovered master and mistress. "Fly-ship go back, an' leave two white mans here?" the black asked.

"What in the world does he mean?" demanded Tom. "Of course we're not going to leave any of our party behind!"

"Let me question him," suggested Mr. Illingway, and he began to talk to the African in his own tongue. A rapid conversation followed, and a look of amazement spread over the faces of the two missionaries, as they listened.

"What is it?" asked Mr. Durban. "What does Tomba say?"

"Why the pygmies have two other white men in captivity," said Mr. Illingway. "They were brought in yesterday, after you were driven away. Two white men, or, rather a white man and a youth, according to Tomba. They are held in one of the huts near where we were, but tied so they couldn't escape in the confusion."

"How does Tomba know this?" asked Mr. Damon.

"He says," translated Mr. Illingway, after more questioning of the black, "that he heard the red pygmies boasting of it after we had escaped. Tomba says he heard them say that, though we were gone, and could not be killed, or sacrificed, the other two captives would meet that horrible fate."

"Two other white captives in the hands of the red imps!" murmured Tom. "We must rescue them!"

"You're not going to turn back now, are you?" asked Mr. Durban.

"No, but I will as soon as I look the ship over. We'll come back to-morrow. And we'll have to make a day attack or it will be too late to save them. Two other white captives! I wonder who they can be."

There was a big surprise in store for Tom Swift.

CHAPTER XXV

THE ROGUE ELEPHANT—CONCLUSION

Early the next day the airship was again afloat. The night, what little of darkness remained after the rescue, had been spent in the clearing in the dense jungle. Some slight repairs had been made to the craft, and it was once more in readiness to be used in battle against the relentless savages.

"We can't wait for darkness," declared Tom. "In the first place there isn't time, and again, we don't know in what part of the village the other captives are. We'll have to hunt around."

"And that means going right down into the midst of the imps and fighting them hand to hand," said Ned.

"That's what it means," assented Tom grimly, "but I guess the powder bombs will help some."

Before starting they had prepared a number of improvised bombs, filled with powder, which could be set off by percussion. It was the plan to drop these down from the airship, into the midst of the savages. When the bomb struck the ground, or even on the bodies of the red dwarfs, it would explode. It was hoped that these would so dismay the little men that they would desert the village, and leave the way clear for a search to be made for the other captives.

On rushed the Black Hawk. There was to be no concealment this time, and Tom did not care how much noise the motors made. Accordingly he turned on full speed.

It was not long before the big plain was again sighted. Everything was in readiness, and the bombs were at hand to be dropped overboard. Tom counted on the natives gathering together in great masses as soon as they sighted the airship, and this would give him the opportunity wanted.

But something different transpired. No sooner was the craft above the village, than from all the huts came pouring out the little red men. But they did not gather together—at least just then. They ran about excitedly, and it could be seen that they were bringing from the huts the rude household utensils in which they did their primitive cooking. The women had their babies, and some, not so encumbered, carried rolls of grass matting. The men had all their weapons.

"Bless my wagon wheel!" cried Mr. Damon. "What's going on?"

"It looks like moving day," suggested Ned Newton.

"That's just what it is!" declared Mr. Durban. "They are going to migrate. Evidently they have had enough of us, and they're going to get out of the neighborhood before we get a chance to do any more damage. They're moving, but where are the white captives?"

He was answered a moment later, for a crowd of the dwarfs rushing to a certain hut, came out leading two persons by means of bark ropes tied about their necks. It was too far off to enable Tom or the others to recognize them, but they could tell by the clothing that they were white captives.

"We've got to save them!" exclaimed the young inventor.

"How?" asked Mr. Damon. And, indeed, it did seem a puzzle for, even as Tom looked, the whole tribe of red imps took up the march into the jungle, dragging the white persons with them. The captives looked up, saw the airship, and made frantic motions for help. It was too far off, yet, to hear their voices. But the distance was lessening every moment, for Tom had speeded the motor to the highest pitch.

"What are you going to do?" demanded Ned.

"I'll show you," answered his chum. "Take some of those bombs, and be ready to drop them overboard when I give the word."

"But we may kill those white people," objected Ned.

"Not the way I'm going to work it. You drop them when I give the word."

Tom steered the airship toward the head of the throng of blacks. The captives were in the rear, and the van of the strange procession was near the edge of the jungle now. Once the red dwarfs got into the tangle of underbrush they could never be found, and their captives would die a miserable death.

"We've got to stop them," murmured Tom. "Are you ready, Ned?"

"Ready!"

"Then drop the bombs!"

Ned dropped them. A sharp explosion was heard, and the head of the procession was blown apart and thrown into confusion. The throng halted.

"Drop more!" cried Tom, sending the ship about in a circle, and hovering it over the middle of the press of savages.

More of the deadly bombs exploded. The pygmies were running about wildly. Tom, who was closely watching the rear of the cavalcade, suddenly called out:

"Now's our chance! They've let their captives go, and are running into the jungle. We must swoop down, and get the prisoners!"

It was no sooner said than the nose of the Black Hawk was pointed downward. Onward it flew, the two captives wildly waving their hands to the rescuers. There was no more danger from the red savages. They had been thrown into panic and confusion, and wore rapidly disappearing into the forest. The terrible weapons of the whites had been too much for them.

"Quick! Get on board!" called Tom, as he brought the machinery to a stop. The airship now rested on the ground, close to the former captives. "Get in here!" shouted the young inventor. "They may change their minds and come back."

The two white persons ran toward the Black Hawk. Then one of them— the smaller—halted and cried out:

"Why, it's Tom Swift!"

Tom turned and glanced at the speaker. A look of astonishment spread over his face.

"Andy Foger—here!" gasped Tom. "How in the world—?"

"I dink besser as ve git on der board, und dalk aftervard!" exclaimed Andy's companion, who spoke with a strong German accent. "I like not dose red little mans."

In another minute the two rescued ones were safe on Tom Swift's airship, and it had arisen high enough to be out of all danger.

"How in the world did you ever get here?" asked Tom of the lad who had so often been his enemy.

"I'll tell you soon," spoke Andy, "but first, Tom, I want to ask your forgiveness for all I've done to you, and to thank you, from the bottom of my heart, for saving us. I thought we were going to be killed by those dwarfs; didn't you, Herr Landbacher?"

"Sure I did. But ve are all right now. Dis machine is efen besser as mine vot vos lost. Is dere anyt'ing to eats, on board, if you vill excuse me for being so bolt as to ask?"

"Plenty to eat," said Tom, laughing, "and while you eat you can tell us your story. And as for you, Andy, I hope we'll be friends from now on," and Tom held out his hand.

There was not much to tell that the reader has not already guessed. Andy and the German, as has been explained, went abroad to give airship flights. They were in the lower part of Egypt, and a sudden gale drove them into Africa.

For a long time they sailed on, and then their fuel gave out, and they had to descend into the jungle. They managed to fall in with some friendly blacks, who treated them well. The airship was useless without gasolene, and it was abandoned.

Andy and the German inventor were planning to walk to some white settlement, when the tribe they were with was attacked by the red dwarfs and vanquished. Andy and his friend were taken prisoners, and carried to the very village where the missionaries were, just before the latter's rescue.

Then came the fight, and the saving of Andy and the German, almost at the last minute.

"Well, you certainly had nearly as many adventures as we did," said Tom. "But I guess they're over now."

But they were not. For several days the airship sailed on over the jungles without making a descent. Mr. and Mrs. Illingway wished to be landed at a white settlement where they had other missionary friends. Tom would go with them. This was done, and Tom and the others spent some time in this place, receiving so many kinds of thanks that they had to protest.

Andy and Herr Landbacher asked to be taken back to the coast, where they could get a steamer to America. Andy was a very different lad now, and not the bully of old.

"Well, hadn't we better be thinking of getting back home?" asked Tom one day.

"Not until we get some more ivory," declared Mr. Durban. "I think we'll have to have another elephant hunt."

They did, about a week later, and got some magnificent tusks. Tom's electric rifle did great work, to the wonder of Andy and Mr. Landbacher, who had never before seen such a curious weapon. They also did some night hunting.

"But we haven't got that pair of extra large tusks that I want," said the old hunter, as he looked at the store of ivory accumulated after the last hunt. "I want those, and then I'll be satisfied. There is one section of the country that we have not touched as yet, and I'd like to visit that."

"Then let's go," proposed Tom, so, good-bys having been said to the missionaries, who sent greetings to their friends in America, and to the church people who had arranged for their rescue, the airship was once more sent to the deepest part of a certain jungle, where Mr. Durban hoped to get what he wanted.

They had another big hunt, but none of the elephants had any remarkable tusks, and the hunter was about to give up in despair, and call the expedition over, when one afternoon, as they were sailing along high enough to merely clear the tops of the trees, Tom heard a great crashing down below.

"There's something there," he called to Mr. Durban. "Perhaps a small herd of elephants. Shall we go down?"

Before Mr. Durban could answer there came into view, in a small clearing, an elephant of such size, and with such an enormous pair of tusks, that the young inventor and the old hunter could not repress cries of astonishment.

"There's your beast!" said Tom. "I'll go down and you can pot him," and, as he spoke, Tom stopped the propellers, so that the ship hung motionless in the air above where the gigantic brute was.

Suddenly, as though possessed by a fit of rage, the elephant rushed at a good-sized tree and began butting it with his head. Then, winding his trunk around it he pulled it up by the roots, and began trampling on it out of a paroxysm of anger.

"A rogue elephant!" exclaimed Mr. Durban. "Don't go down if you value your life, or the safety of the airship. If we attacked that brute on the ground, we would be the hunted instead of the hunters. That's a rogue elephant of the worst kind, and he's at the height of his rage."

This was indeed so, for the beast was tearing about the clearing like mad, breaking off trees, and uprooting them in sheer wantonness. Tom knew what a "rogue" elephant was. It is a beast that goes away from the herd, and lives solitary and alone, attacking every living thing that comes in his way. It is a species of madness, a disease which attacks elephants and sometimes passes away. More often the afflicted creature gives battle to everything and every animal he meets until he is killed or carried off by his malady. It was such an elephant that Tom now saw, and he realized what the hunter said about attacking one, as he saw the brute's mad rushes.

"Well, if it's dangerous to attack him on the ground, we'll kill him from up above," said the young inventor. "Here is the electric rifle, Mr. Durban. I'll let you have the honor of getting those tusks. My! But they're whoppers! Better use almost a full charge. Don't take any chances on merely wounding him, and having him rush off to the jungle."

"I won't," said the old hunter, and he adjusted the electric rifle which Tom handed him.

As the great beast was tearing around, trumpeting shrilly and breaking off trees Mr. Durban fired. The creature sank down, instantly killed, and was out of his misery, for often it is great pain which makes an otherwise peaceable elephant become a "rogue."

"He's done for," said Ned. "I guess you have the tusks you want now, Mr. Durban."

"I think so," agreed the hunter, and when the airship was sent down, and the ivory cut out, it was found that the tusks were even larger than they had supposed. "It is a prize worth having," said Mr. Durban. "I'm sure my customer will think so, too. Now I'm ready to head for the coast."

Tom Swift went to the engine room, while the last big tusks were being stored away with the other ivory. Several parts of the motor needed oiling, and Ned was assisting in this work.

"Going to start soon?" asked Mr. Durban, appearing in the doorway.

"Yes; why?" inquired Tom, who noted an anxious note in the voice of the hunter.

"Well, I don't like staying longer in this jungle than I can help. It's not healthy in the first place, and then it's a wild and desolate place, where all sorts of wild beasts are lurking, and where wandering hands of natives may appear at any time."

"You don't mean that the red pygmies will come back; do you?" asked Ned.

"There's no telling," replied Mr. Durban with a shrug of his shoulders. "Only, as long as we've got what we're after, I'd start off as soon as possible."

"Yes, don't run any chances with those little red men," begged Andy Foger, who had given himself up for lost when he and his companion fell into their hands.

"Radder vould I be mit cannibals dan dose little imps!" spoke the German fervently.

"We'll start at once," declared Tom. "Are you all aboard, and is everything loaded into the airship?"

"Everything. I guess." answered Mr. Anderson.

Tom looked to the motor, saw that it was in working order, and shoved over the lever of the gas machine to begin the generating of the lifting vapor. To his surprise there was no corresponding hiss that told of the gas rushing into the bag.

"That's odd," he remarked. "Ned, see if anything is wrong with that machine. I'll pull the lever again."

The bank clerk stood beside the apparatus, while Tom worked the handle, but whatever was the matter with it was too intricate or complicated for Ned to solve.

"I can't see what ails it," he called to his chum. "You better have a peep."

"All right, I'll look if you work the handle."

The passengers on the airship, which now rested in a little clearing in the dense jungle, gathered at the engine room door, looking at Tom and Ned as they worked over the machine.

"Bless my pulley wheel!" exclaimed Mr. Damon "I hope nothing has gone wrong."

"Well something has!" declared the young inventor in a muffled voice, for he was down on his hands and knees peering under the gas apparatus. "One of the compression cylinders has cracked," he added dubiously. "It must have snapped when we landed this last time. I came down too heavily."

"What does that mean?" asked Mr. Durban, who did not know much about machinery.

"It means that I've got to put a new cylinder in," went on Tom. "It's quite a job, too, but we can't make gas without it!"

"Well, can't you do it just as well up in the air as down here?" asked Mr. Durban. "Make an ascension, Tom, and do the repairs up above, where we've got good air, and where—"

He paused suddenly, and seemed to be listening.

"What is it?" asked the young inventor quickly. There was no need to answer, for, from the jungle without, came the dull booming of the war drums of some natives.

"That's what I was afraid of!" cried the old elephant hunter, catching up his gun. "Some black scout has seen us and is summoning his tribesmen. Hurry, Tom, send up the ship, and we'll take care of the savages."

"But I CAN'T send her up!" cried Tom.

"You can't? Why not?"

"Because the gas machine won't work until I put in a new cylinder, and that will take at least a half a day."

"Go up as an aeroplane then!" cried Mr. Damon. "Bless my monkey wrench, Tom, you've often done it before."

For answer Tom waved his hand toward the thick jungle all about them.

"We haven't room to get a running start of ten feet," he said, "and without a start the airship can never rise as a mere aeroplane. The only way we can get up from the jungle is like a balloon, and without the gas—"

He paused significantly. The sound of the war drums became louder, and to it was added a weird singing chant.

"The natives!" cried Mr. Anderson. "They're coming right this way! We must fight them off if they attack us!"

"Where's the electric rifle?" asked Ned. "Get that out, Tom!"

"Wait!" suggested Mr. Durban. "This is serious! It looks as if they were going to attack us, and they have us at a disadvantage. Our only safety is in flight, but as Tom says we can't go up until the gas machine is fixed, he will have to attend to that part of it while we keep off the black men. Tom, we can't spare you to fight this time! You repair the ship as soon as you can, and we'll guard her from the natives. And you've got to work lively!"

"I will!" cried the young inventor. "It's luck we have a spare cylinder!"

Suddenly there was a louder shout in the jungle and it was followed by a riot of sound. War drums were beaten, tom-toms clashed and the natives howled.

"Here they are!" cried Mr. Anderson.

"Bless my suspenders!" shouted Mr. Damon. "Where is my gun?"

"Here, you take mine, and I'll use the electric rifle," answered the elephant hunter. As he spoke there was a hissing sound in the air and a flight of spears passed over the airship.

The defenders slipped outside, while Tom, with Ned to help him, worked feverishly to repair the break. They were in a serious strait, for with the airship practically helpless they were at the mercy of the natives. And as Tom glanced momentarily from the window, he saw scores of black, half-naked forms slipping in and out among the trees and trailing vines.

Soon the rifles of his friends began to crack, and the yells of the natives were changed to howls of anguish. The electric weapon, though it made no noise, did great execution.

"I only hope they don't puncture the gas bag," murmured Tom, as he began taking the generating machine apart so as to get out the cracked cylinder.

"If they do, it's all up with us," murmured Ned.

After their first rush, finding that the white men were on the alert, the blacks withdrew some distance, where their spears and arrows were not so effective. Our friends, including Andy Foger, and the German, kept up a hot fire whenever a skulking black form could be seen.

But, though the danger from the spears and arrows was less, a new peril presented itself. This was from the blow guns. The curious weapons shot small arrows, tipped with tufts of a cottony substance in place of feathers, and could be sent for a long distance. The barbs were not strong enough to pierce the tough fabric of the gas bag, as a spear or arrow would have done, but there was more danger from them to our friends who were on deck.

"Those barbs may be poisoned," said Mr. Durban, "and in case any one is wounded, the wound, though it be but a scratch, must be treated with antiseptics. I have some."

This course was followed, the elephant hunter being wounded twice, and Andy Foger and Mr. Damon once each. There was not a native to be seen now, for they were hiding behind the trees of the jungle, but every now and then a blowgun barb would whizz out of the forest.

Finally Mr. Durban suggested that they erect improvised shelters, behind which they could stand with their rifle, and breastworks were made out of packing boxes. Then our friends were comparatively safe. But they had to be on the alert, and it was nervous work, for they could not tell what minute the blacks would rush from the jungle, and, in spite of the fire from the electric rifle and other guns, overwhelm the ship.

It was very trying to Tom and Ned, for they had to work hard and rapidly in the close engine room. The sweat dripped down off them, but they kept at it. It was three hours before the broken cylinder was removed, and it was no light task to put in the other, for the valves had to be made very tight to prevent leakage.

The two lads stopped to get something to eat, while the guards kept sharp watch against a surprise. At intervals came a flight of barbs, and occasionally a black form could be seen, when it was instantly fired at. Several times the barbaric noise of the tom-toms and war drums, with which the shouts of the natives mingled, broke out deafeningly.

"Think you can repair it by night?" asked Mr. Durban anxiously of Tom.

"I hope so," was the response.

"Because if we have to stay here after dark—well, I don't want to do it if I can help it," finished the hunter.

Neither did the young inventor, and he redoubled his efforts to make the repairs. It was getting dark when the last belt was in place, and it was high time, too, for the natives were getting bolder, creeping up through the forest to within shooting distance with their arrows and spears.

"There!" cried Tom at length. "Now we'll see if she works!" Once more he pulled the starting lever, and this time there was the welcome hiss of the gas.

"Hurrah!" cried Ned.

The young inventor turned the machine on at full power. In a few minutes the Black Hawk trembled through her length.

"She's going up! Bless my balloon basket! She's going up!" cried Mr. Damon.

The natives must have suspected that something unusual was going on, for they made a sudden rush, yelling and beating their drums. Mr. Durban and the others hurried out on deck and fired at them, but there was little more need. With a bound the airship left the earth, being rapidly carried up by the gas. The blacks sent a final shower of spears after her, but only one was effective, slightly wounding the German. Then Tom started the motor, the propellers whizzed, and the Black Hawk was once more under way, just as night settled over the jungle, and upon the horde of black and howling savages that rushed around, maddened over the escape of their intended victims.

No further accidents marred the trip to the coast, which was reached in due time, and very glad our friends were to be away from the jungle and the land of the red pygmies.

A division was made of the ivory, and Tom's share was large enough to provide him with a substantial amount. Ned and Mr. Damon were also given a goodly sum from the sale of the tusks. The big ones, from the "rogue," were shipped to the man who had commissioned Mr. Durban to secure them for him.

"Well, now for home," said Tom, when the airship had been taken apart for shipment. "I guess you'll be glad to get back to the United States, won't you, friends?"

"That's what," agreed Andy Foger. "I think I'm done with airships. Ugh! When I think of those red dwarfs I can't sleep nights!"

"Yah, dot iss so!" agreed the German.

"Well, I'm going to settle down for a time," declared Tom. "I've had enough adventures for a while, but those in elephant land—"

But Tom Swift was not done with adventures, and what farther happened to him may be learned by reading the next volume of this series, which will be entitled, "Tom Swift in the City of Gold; or, Marvelous Adventures Underground."

They all made a safe and pleasant voyage home, and as news of the rescue of the missionaries had been cabled to America, Tom and his friends were met, as they left the steamer, by a crowd of newspaper reporters, who got a good story of the battle with the red pygmies, though Tom was inclined to make light of his part in the affair.

"Now for Shopton, home, Dad, Eradicate Sampson and his mule!" exclaimed Tom, as they boarded a train in New York.

"And somebody else, too, I guess; eh?" asked Ned of his chum, with a laugh.

"That's none of your affair!" declared Tom, as he blushed, and then he, too, joined in the merriment.

And now, for a time, we will say good-by to the young inventor and his friends.